Catc

By

Jordan Silver

Table of Contents

Chapter 1

Mancini

I felt the burn in my muscles, as I lifted the two hundred and fifty pound weights for my last rep; this is just what I needed to take my mind off of the fuckery I have to deal with later. I've found over the years, that if I push my body hard enough, my mind goes into what I call 'phase'. I can put everything else aside and concentrate on the task at hand. It's just one of the ways I've taught myself to have total control.

There's no one else around to distract me at this early hour, as I'm in my personal state of the art gym, on the thirty-third floor of my high-rise building. Though the room is covered wall to wall with mirrors, I do not watch myself. That is not what this is about; this is about control.

In a few hours, I'll be sitting down across from what's believed to be one of the world's foremost criminals, a little less known fact by any who aren't part of the law enforcement communities of the world. He's wanted by almost every leading government agency for questioning, but still he walks free, then again so am I.

The thought brought a sinister grin to my face; I loved pitting my brain and skills against the best they had to offer. I haven't met one who could best me thus far, which was a bane for them I'm sure, and just more fodder for my kicks and laughs folder.

Sweat formed on my brow and across my shoulders, as I pushed my body just that much harder; next up, stretches and I'm good for the day. An hour of hard exercise always sets me up for the rest of the day, invigorating.

My phone rang, causing me to ease down the heaviness from my hands; I found the first smile of the day as I saw the name on the readout. I flexed my arms and shook it out, prepared to cut my session short for one of the only people in the world I thought worthy of my time.

"Mama..."

"Don't you mama me Hank Mancini, where have you been? I don't see you three whole days, no phone call no nothing, maybe you're dead, I don't know, how would I know? Nobody tells me anything, why you treat your mother this way Hank, didn't I take care of you as a boy?"

I rolled my eyes as she went on with her usual guilt trip, not uttering a word, until she wound down. It was always the same with mama, she's all of five feet, but you'd swear with her gumption, that she was six feet tall. She's the only human being on the face of the earth that had the power to bring me to heel as she puts it.

"First of all you're lying mama, I spoke to you yesterday morning. I told you I had a very busy schedule and you said dad was taking you out to some fancy do and you had a full day planned at the spa, so you would be in and out all day getting ready, ring a bell?"

"Oh that was you? I thought it was Jaxxon or Adrien, or maybe Jace, pfft, I can't keep my boys straight anymore."

"You know mama, if I wasn't so strong of heart I'd be jealous."

"Yeah, yeah, yeah, you've been saying that for twenty years now my son; so tell me, what badness are you getting up to today?"

I didn't answer, she knew I never discussed my business with her, but that didn't stop her from asking. A long time ago, I'd had to let her in on a little of who her son had become. But that was the one and only time, and only because some things had transpired that had necessitated me sharing some information with her and dad. Since then, I'd made damn sure I never needed to involve them any farther.

I liked to keep my personal and professional lives separate. I'd better; it could mean a matter of life or death to those who mattered most. Though both of my surrogate brothers had joined law enforcement agencies, it was not quite the same thing, but just as dangerous all the same. At least mama was an equal opportunity worrier; she worried about all of us.

Something I hated, but could see no way around. I imagined her sitting in her solarium, having her morning coffee, as she enjoyed her plant life and deciding which of her children to terrorize next. I'll have to go see my favorite girl soon, it had been at least a week since the last time, and if I didn't go to her, the little tyrant would show up here, laden down with a week's worth of food and rearrange my house to the way she thought it should look. Gotta love my mama.

I messed around on the phone for a few minutes with my favorite girl, before tossing it back to the chair where I kept it. I'd have to remember to get her something nice, it's been a while and mama does enjoy her gifts; and the men in her life kept her well supplied. Hopefully, she was already busy interrogating one of them, because when she got into this mood I knew what was coming next.

My thoughts went from family to death in the blink of an eye; in my line of work, death and darkness, was never too far from the surface. I literally swam with the filth of the world, day in and day out; have been for quite some time now, and it didn't look like I would be stopping anytime soon.

There was always some shit going on, in some corner of the world that needed my brand of expertise. I finished out my routine and headed for the shower. I have a meet downtown later in the afternoon, after my sit down with Jace, that I needed to be on point for.

The fucking Feds are acting up again, like I gave a fuck; they're nothing more than annoying little gnats, buzzing around my ass. But I've become an expert at avoiding their overpaid, underachieving asses for the past ten years. I might have admired their tenacity had I not been the one on the receiving end of their bullshit, but all I felt was total disdain. At least they were consistent if nothing else, the fucks.

Their last attempt at throwing me behind bars and throwing away the key had ended with the termination of that particular agent's career for fabrication of evidence. They couldn't pin any of the one hundred and one crimes they suspected me of on me through legal channels, so he'd decided to get creative. Too bad for him, I wasn't one to be fucked with and I had the money and the resources to fight back. Now his pals at the bureau were out for blood; too fucking bad, I have no interest in donating.

"Fuck, what is this, Grand Central?" Fucking phone is a pain in the ass this morning. Most people knew not to bother me at this time, unless it was an emergency; of course that didn't apply to mama, nothing ever did. I answered without first checking the readout.

"Mancini."

"Hank, where the hell have you been? I've been calling and calling for the past three days, do you know who I am...?"

I took the phone away from my ear and pressed end. Chick lost her damn mind; I turned it off when it started ringing again. That ought to send the message home loud and clear, once and for all. Hank Mancini bowed to no one, get the fuck outta here.

I threw on my Armani gear. Today was businessman suave. Crisp white shirt, opened at the collar, under a steel grey suit, no tie, I hate those shits. I think the fuck who invented them had some type of auto erotic asphyxiation fetish, and found the perfect way to hang the fuck out of himself all day, getting his jollies, while fooling the world that his creation was the next best thing in fashion.

I barely passed a comb through my unruly black curls, because the shit did its own thing anyway, no matter what I did, so why bother? Opening my watch safe, I perused my collection, before settling on a Breitling. I checked the shine on my shoes and was ready to go in less than half an hour. Tomorrow I'll probably be in sweats and ten year old runners, but that's just me, it's the life I live and I have the money and the prestige to do whatever the fuck I want.

I felt eyes on me from the moment I stepped out of the building. I didn't know who had me in their cross hairs this week, Interpol, FBI, SSI or who the fuck. Sometimes it was one or the other, or sometimes they got enterprising and teamed up. It must piss them off that they could only watch me from afar these days, since I'd fought and won that battle too, the first and only time the fucks had tried to put eyes and ears inside one of my places. Now, by law they were prohibited from doing what the good judge had termed 'harassing a citizen of the USA'.

It was barely eight o'clock in the morning and it was already ninety degrees in the shade. Another scorcher, just what I needed to round out my fucked up day. I took a cursory glance around, playing my game of spot the spook. Sometimes I gave them a little wave just to fuck with them. The last two I had actually ordered pizzas, while they sat outside my place like the paparazzi stalking a little starlet. According to the delivery guy, they almost shit themselves, and after questioning him extensively, until they were satisfied he was really just a pizza delivery guy and not a criminal mastermind, they'd let him go; they'd kept the pizzas.

I climbed into the back of my waiting car, another Breitling creation, after spotting the jackasses in a town car three doors down; and headed to my first stop of the day. Traffic was a little more sedate in my neighborhood on Central Park West, which would change just a few short streets over, where the hustle and bustle of the city began.

I own clubs all over the city, as well as internationally, along with a few restaurants and one oil-company down in Texas. I have my fingers in a lot of pies yes, and it amazes me that I can control it all, with just the push of a button. Technology has gone a long way in making life easier for guys like me. I could sit in a pied-a-terre in Paris France and conduct business in Prague, gotta love it.

Some business still needed to be handled the old fashioned way though, face to face; though I tried to keep those to a minimum, because people got on my fucking nerves. On the phone, or behind the computer screen, I could hang up or log off; in person, I usually ended up having to fight the urge to cold clock a motherfucker. Sometimes I wasn't so good at reining it in, it came with the territory.

The clubs fit in perfectly with my lifestyle. They were a nice backdrop and a nice meeting place for my other dealings, this way I always stayed in control of my environment. I had shit set up so my stalkers couldn't come sniffing around, especially in this particular place.

Mancini's had been my first foray into the nightclub business. As with everything else, I'd done the homework, looked at the pros and cons from all angles, and dove right on in. My brothers were part owners with me in all my ventures, because that's the way I wanted it. I never did anything business-wise without involving them, and at the rate they were procreating, they were going to need every dime.

I usually tried to touch base with each of my places at least once a week, if not more, whenever I was stateside; although I had eyes and ears in every one of them. I liked knowing what was going on in my place; who was doing what. Only select areas were off limits for my listening devices, unless I changed that for my own purposes. These were the places where I conducted the business the police of the world would like to know about, and in fact have been trying their damnedest to uncover for at least ten years now.

At thirty-four I'd done plenty to garner their attention. I flaunted my prowess, while thumbing my nose at them and each time I bested one of their agencies, they ran with their tails tucked between their legs; until they regrouped and came back at me harder than before.

Too bad none of it ever worked. I had no interest in sitting in a cell, but neither did I have any interest in playing nice with the good old boys. They'd have to work for every morsel, and I threw them none. So far they were o for plenty; some of them had made for great entertainment over the years, some not so much. But each time they got to be too bothersome, I flung them off like the pesky insects they were.

Sitting in my office, on the top floor of one of my three nightclubs in this area of the Meatpacking district, I went over the night's take from the day before. Not bad for a Wednesday night, but then again, none of my places ever did poorly. Good promo, and the off chance that the man himself might make an appearance on any given night, kept my places packed. Though there's been lots of speculation in the news media over the years about my shadowy lifestyle outside the limelight, people still seemed obsessed with who I am and everyone wanted a piece of me.

I gave them little nibbles, but never enough to sate their appetites; I'm not stupid, that's what kept them coming back for more. Women, not to sound clichéd, were a dime a dozen, I had my pick, but I'm very choosy. Over the years I've sampled a select few. In my younger years, I even gorged myself there for a while, but now my tastes were changing. The older I got, it seemed the less enticing the lure of the chase became.

Not that I was looking for permanence or anything like that, but I've grown tired of playing the field. My mama would love nothing better, than to see her one remaining son hogtied, and spitting out little Mancinis to her heart's content. But as much as I hate disappointing her, this was the one thing I'd yet to give her, and things didn't look like they would be changing anytime soon. I'd acquired a healthy dose of distrust in my travels; it would take a very special woman to break down those walls.

Of course I couldn't be here without being interrupted, so the knock at the door fifteen minutes later was no big surprise.

"Come in." I barely took my eyes off of what I was doing, as one of my day managers came in. Starling was supermodel beautiful, with the looks

JORDAN SILVER | 21

and the body to make it on any runway in the world, but preferred to have the life she led. Working for me during the day, and being at home with her husband and kids at night.

"What's up Star?"

"You flew the coop again didn't you Hanky?"

I wish she'd stop calling me that shit; she's the only one who does and no matter how much I threatened her with termination and all manner of bodily harm, she refused to relent. I chose to ignore her disrespect and focused instead on her cryptic question, the girl's nuts so who knew what the hell she was talking about.

"What're you talking about now?"

She rolled her eyes at me and huffed, which seemed to be her trademark move when dealing with yours truly.

"Your latest cuckoo puff, she's been making the rounds, because Sabra and Annette already called to complain about her behavior. Now me, I just told the nut that I'm not your damn answering service and that was the end of that, but the others aren't nearly as brave as I am, so they've been suffering through her bullshit."

"I guess we're talking about Mara here?"

"Yep, so what did you do this time, the bracelet, the watch, the necklace what?"

"None of the above; I've just been really busy lately; now what's going on with my business?"

"You're cold dude, straight up icicle; anyway then, on to more important things apparently. Let's see, sales are good, business is booming, in spite of the recession. Mostly bored debutantes, with daddy's platinum card burning a hole in their pockets, sipping on thirty-dollar martinis and nibbling on twenty-dollar veggie wraps. That about sums it up, oh and I need a raise." She grinned at me.

" I just gave your ass an undeserved raise, two months ago, and your disdain is showing again." For someone who was once a debutante herself, she sure didn't feel any love for her fellow ilk. She positively abhorred women of a certain class, including her own mother on occasion. According to her, they were all bubble headed nymphets; that could be due to her mother divorcing her father when she was thirteen years old to marry up.

"Meh! Whatever! Anyway, you need to deal with the beer distributors. People are complaining about the beer on tap, they say it's a bit watered-down. We checked the pressurc and everything's fine there, so the only thing we can deduce, is that it's a problem originating from the company. I've been hearing whispers from other places in the city that seems to be having the same issue, so I'm thinking you might want to jump on that right quick." She fiddled with the stuff on my desk, until I rapped her knuckles with my Mont Blanc.

I hope for their sakes they weren't trying to screw me over, I pay top dollar for premium beer, because that's what the people who come into my places expect. If I find that my distributor was playing me that would mean finding another reputable one. This fucking recession was turning everyone into fucking criminals; I hate shoddy business dealings, fuck. But it's part of the world sadly; see that's why I can't stand people, fucking dishonest assholes.

"Sure anything else?"

"Nope, that's about it, the numbers are on the spreadsheet; I don't know if you want to deal with orders since you're here, otherwise I've got it covered."

"You do that; what about the floor, any problems in house?"

"Nah, we're cruising along just fine. We don't ever really have any problems there, except for when one of the newbies get a look at you and fall for your piercing eyes and your handsome self; then it takes a few months for them to get over the heartbreak when they realize you don't shit where you eat and never will."

"Go to work Star, I don't know how my brother puts up with that mouth of yours."

"He loves it." She grinned at me again, always full of piss and vinegar this one.

"Spare me please; one of you better call mama, she's on the warpath again, something about not seeing her grandkids lately and, you know the deal."

"Must be Jaxx and Sabra, Adrien and I were just over there like two nights ago, before he left town."

"Well you know how she is, she needs daily if not hourly contact; the woman is relentless. I'd appreciate it if the rest of you could keep her off my ass with this grand kids shit. You'd think after the fifty or so you and Adrien and Sabra and Jaxx gave her she'd be satisfied, but no."

"Uh huh, Mara not the motherly type?"

"Out!" She laughed her ass off as she left. I checked my watch; I still had a few hours left before my first meet. I got the books in order. I'll be able to pay the mortgage for the next little while at least. That was a running joke between me and the boys whenever we made another couple hundred grand or so. Shit, the way things were going; we might not be too far off the mark. Man has totally fucked shit up; we were headed for a collision course with imminent disaster, and still people didn't learn, didn't stop in their tracks and say, 'hey, what can I do to make this shit better'?

Glancing over at the security monitor, I caught sight of my brother Jaxxon entering the place; we didn't have any plans for today as far as I knew, so something must be up.

He came in and eyed me like I'd done something wrong, which wasn't anything new. My brothers were always giving me the gimlet eye; they claimed my line of work made their lives unnecessarily difficult. They wanted me to take it easy on their peers, but I refused to, I was having way too much fun keeping them on their toes.

"You gonna say something, or just stand there and give me the stink eye?"

Jaxx ran his hand through his shaggy, dark brown hair, which he wore to his shoulders these days. That'll last until mama got after him about his grooming habits as she calls it, and to please her, he'll lop most of it off.

"Well little brother, don't' you have criminals to catch? FBI having an off day or some shit?"

Chapter 2

"Nice to see you too brother."

"What's up lil brother, I didn't know we had plans today, did I miss something?"

"Nah, I just wanted to come by and give you a heads up about something."

"Fuck, your boss on my ass again now too? I thought after the last time it'd take him at least another three months before he ventured back into the ring again."

"Very funny bro, you sure you don't want to retire early? Take that boat of yours on an around the world cruise or something?"

"Nah I'm having too much fun; so what is it this time?"

"Listen, seriously bro, they're putting someone new on you, of course I've not been privy to the details, but Adrien overheard something on his end and passed it on, so I could give you a heads up. He's still out of town or he would've told you himself, but no one can ever get ahold of you."

"Who is it this time another profiler, those fucks still profiling my ass?"

"Nah, I think they've pretty much figured out that you're mentally fucked already. It is a profiler, only I'm not sure what angle they're playing with this one."

"So...who is it, anyone I might know?"

"Nope, she's a newbie, Cierra Stone."

"A chick? They're putting a chick on me? What, did I come down on the most wanted list or some shit, who knocked me off?"

"Nah you still reign supreme, but she's supposedly the best mind they've seen in twenty years."

"At least that's something; I still warrant the best."

"You're sick you know that?"

"So what does she look like?"

"Dog I don't know, I just caught a glimpse of her freshman picture after Adrien mentioned it, she's young; still got that Quantico shine on her, fresh off the farm."

"What's Durant thinking putting a little dove like that on me? He knows I'll eat her ass for breakfast, unless they've upped their game; she got great legs?"

"I already told you jackass, I don't know what she looks like. She hasn't landed yet, sometime in the next day or two she'll be here. Anyway, that's all I've got so far, I'll keep you in the loop if I learn anything else. Right now I gotta go bro, I've got an asshole sneaking arms into my city from the Carolinas of all places. Why the fuck these states can't get together and have one governing law so jurisdiction bullshit does not apply, I'll never know. One fucking country and a hundred and ten differing laws, catch you later."

"Hey Jaxx...sorry." I didn't have to explain; he knew exactly what I was getting at.

"Don't start that shit again Hank." He turned back at the door.

"I can't, I know they're holding you back because of your association with me..."

"And I told you before I don't care about that."

"But if you severed ties..."

"Fuck it Hank no, not gonna happen, we may not share blood, but we're brothers in every way that counts and we're going to stay brothers."

"Yes, I understand, but it's holding you back." And that fucked with me, I had to do what I do, no doubt about it. It was one of those necessary evil type things, but the fact that it hindered my brothers in their chosen fields, was something I struggled with on occasion. It was the only way law enforcement has been able to get to me thus far.

"I'm not having this conversation with you bro, so just drop it; family's family, they don't like my family, fuck them."

"Speaking of which, how are my little sister and my niece and nephews?"

"The little terrors are running around driving us crazy, and Sabra's hanging in there. She did say you're a hard task master and the first chance she gets, she's breaking a foot off in your ass."

"Whatever, your wife and your sister in law loves to bitch about everything, then after they've implemented my ideas and see how much easier and smoother things run, they want to coo at me. Anyway, I have to come by, I got some new shit for the boys."

"Oh no you don't, you're not bringing over any new gifts until I vet them first."

"What, what'd I do?"

"What did you do, drum sets? You gave a three and a four-year-old drum sets, the fuck you think has been going on in my house?"

I laughed my ass off.

"Get outta here, I'll be by sometime this week, I think lil Jeff said he wanted a python."

"I'll fucking kill you you do that shit bro, I'll be doing the bureau a favor."

"I'll tell ma you said that shit."

"Mean, just dog mean."

"Later lil brother."

"Later bro."

Fucking FBI, those fucks stay on me like a lion on a rhino's ass. One of these days they're gonna piss me the fuck off for real, and I'll give their bitch asses something to cry about, dumb fucks. So far I've mostly been playing with the different agencies, foreign and domestic, that try keeping tabs on me. It was fun outwitting them at every turn, but they've all learnt in some capacity or the other not to go too far. I valued my freedom too much to have them trampled by a bunch of blowhards, who were sometimes almost as corrupt as the fucks they were supposed to be putting away.

I opened up my laptop and typed in the series of numbers needed to get me into the FBI database undetected. These fucks were so busy hounding my every step that they'd left their left flank unprotected. It was comical how fucking easy it was to breach their security. I've been accessing most, if not all, of the delicate top-secret information of most government agencies, for the better part of eight years, ever since I'd learned the fine art of hacking from a master.

You see the thing with me, is that I'm a one- man team. I like working alone as much as possible when handling a job. If I needed information, I would rather be able to get it myself, as opposed to having to wait on someone else to get it for me. So I'd trained with the best and picked up some of my own tricks along the way.

Now these days I'm better than my teacher, but not only that, since I'd mastered the art of hacking, I'd learned how to safeguard myself against the same. It'd take them years to crack my codes and by then, I would've changed them once more, so they'd just have to start all over again. I'm sure it was a great source of frustration for them. Dumb fucks.

I went through the now familiar channels that I used whenever I was spying on them spying on me. Jaxxon had given me her name, so it was no hardship finding her in their database. I felt the jolt, but didn't think anything of it, just a quick hit to the heart and gut that was too fleeting to really register.

"There she is, fuck me…come to daddy."

Chapter 3

Cierra

I made it; hard to believe, after all the ups and downs and turmoil, but I'm finally where I wanted to be. It's been an uphill battle, but all worth it. Now I can fight for justice, for those who deserved it, and fulfill a childhood promise, made so long ago on a lonely hilltop in Maryland, all at the same time.

I pulled my thick black curls back and secured them at my nape. My hair is a bloody nuisance half the time, but I could never go much shorter than shoulder length. Maybe because that's how I remember mom wearing hers when I was a kid, before she was taken so suddenly and horrifically from me.

"So what do you think Cierra, is this our guy?" The voice breaking into my little trip down memory lane brought me back to the present, and the task at hand. The room was close and just a little stuffy, as most rooms of its ilk tend to be. There were men scattered around a long table, with computer screens up and running, papers scattered haphazardly over every available surface.

The peeling walls really could do with a touch up, and the floors were scuffed, but for some reason, this was my place of solace. It was in this room and others like it here on the farm, where I got to hone my skills. This is where my dream of justice drew closer to reality.

Not many knew of my true purpose for being here, at least I hoped not. And I wouldn't want them to find out; that might stand in my way, others might not understand and I couldn't risk that. My mind is my greatest asset, my handlers have taken to calling it their secret weapon. I don't know how or why it works the way it does, I just know that it fits in perfectly with what I had to do; the one thing of importance in my otherwise bleak world.

I took my time and studied the subject again; couldn't be too rash here. A mistake now could mean the difference between life and death.

Frank Connell had already murdered eleven people, or so it appeared. The profile suggested our perp was a loner, between the ages of thirty and forty-five. Who probably still lived at home with his mother, had poor social skills, and an intense hatred of women.

Profiling had been in existence for decades now and anyone with a grain of sense knew that there was always room for human error, or they should. I guess one of the reasons I was being hailed as the next best thing to pass through these vaunted halls, is because I'd turned profiling on its ear. Instead of going with the textbook, I went outside the box and worked my way back in.

I've studied plenty cases, where the profiler had been wrong; I'd even been the catalyst that led to the freeing of two men, who had been wrongfully convicted and sitting on death row. This was all while I was still in school and working as a volunteer for an organization that specialized in reviewing questionable convictions.

That's why I'm here, well one of the reasons anyway. It was passing strange, that on my quest to imprison the guilty, I started out by freeing the innocent. The fact that I'd gone on to correctly profile and bring about the capture of both actual guilty parties is what had fast-tracked me to Quantico. I'd caught the attention of my intended target; it'd just been a few years earlier than I'd anticipated.

Now I studied the man on the screen, as he'd sat in interview, being grilled by two of our best. I watched body language, eye movement, and perspiration levels. I looked for any nervous twitches and listened to the intonations in his voice and how he responded to certain questions. I wasn't feeling it; the others had already passed judgment; my fellow profilers were sure that this was our guy, but something just wasn't ringing true for me.

There was just something missing I guess, and I've learned to follow my instincts, no matter what was the most popular opinion. We've been working on this particular case for a few weeks already and everyone wanted to be done with it, but not at the expense of a human life. A man's freedom was at stake, a rash decision by the ones who were supposed to be the keepers of justice's gates, would not only be unjust, it would be criminal in the extreme.

Not every middle-aged man who lived at home with mom was a maniacal murderer, and what our guy had done to those women, took not only time and planning, but a heavy dose of hate. That kind of hate was not as easy to hide as the perpetrators thought. When in close proximity you could almost smell it coming off of them.

In observation, I saw it in the eyes; the eyes became almost feral after shedding that much blood. At least that's what I saw. I had no way of knowing what my colleagues saw, or how they went about drawing the conclusions they did, so I just focused on what my brain was telling me and shut out all the white noise around me.

Like any wild animal that hunted, once they tasted of human flesh, they craved it and actively sought it out henceforth. It was the same with the human predator, once he, or she had gotten a taste for murder, or whatever their crime of choice happened to be; it was hard for them to stop. With the animal you could tell the difference, by the change in their behavior; it was the same with man.

This was my secret, a little kernel of truth that had come to me during the darkness of night, one long ago night. I'd still been a young, impressionable girl; still the lost child, who was alone in the world. I stayed up nights, afraid to close my eyes, afraid of what the darkness would hold. Not because of the boogeyman no, my nightmare had been of a different nature. It was at night that I realized I couldn't remember their faces. Gradually they were fading away from my memory.

I'd had no mementos left, no keepsakes. In the chaos of being spirited away in the dead of night, from the home of the friend I'd been staying over with that night, no one had thought to even ask. Then as the weeks went by, when it wasn't certain who had been the target of the massacre and if I was still in danger, all thought of such things got lost in the shuffle.

So it was, that while others my age, were out having fun and doing the growing pains thing, going to parties with friends, enjoying the normal teenage proclivities, I'd been studying human behaviors. I taught myself to look beyond the expected, to push my mind harder. It was as though I went to a different plane of existence, where everything became clearer.

It was almost like pieces to a puzzle, that had been scattered about haphazardly; and I had to painstakingly put it all back together. When I first noticed that nine times out of ten I'd been on point, I decided to use that as my passport into the bureau. From that first compulsion, I made it my mission to hone my skills.

I ate, slept and lived anything to do with crime solving.

I had no idea then, what a profiler was, had no idea where I would fit. I just knew I needed to be here, where I had access to the information that might come in handy, and so I'd pushed myself in every way. That's why today I'm being touted as the best new brain to hit the farm in decades. Some were even saying I was the best ever, and I guess there was some truth to it, since I was offered a position that usually took years of hard work to achieve. I didn't let accolades go to my head though, that's not why I was here; my purpose had never changed, not once in all these years.

So I've stayed true to myself and focused on my goals. I'm not in this for praise and recognition; truth be known if I could be left alone to do what I do, with no one looking over my shoulder, or critiquing, I would be happy. But that's not the way it works. I've been vetted, studied, interrogated, all but put under hypnosis to extract my secrets. One enterprising scientist even joked that he'd like to get a look inside my brain; too bad I'd have to be dead for that happy occurrence to take place.

The others were getting restless waiting for my answer. They'd learned by now, that I wasn't one to be rushed, but that didn't stop them moaning and groaning. I looked up and around the table at the faces gathered there, a sea of male faces; some of them I knew, resented my presence here. Some saw it as unfair that I'd been moved ahead, there'd even been rumors of me sleeping my way here, which had all been quelled when my skills were made evident in exercise after exercise.

"It's not him." I'd known the answer for quite some time now, I'd gone over the case relentlessly and every time I came back to the same thing. Yes he fit the profile, too perfectly and as I've said before, profiles can be wrong. They're compiled by human beings after all, and contrary to what the movies portray, no one is right a hundred percent of the time; not unless he's also capable of walking on water.

"Aww come on Stone; we got the guy dead to rights. He fits the profile to a T. All roads point to him. We even found his DNA at the last scene."

"Stodgy DNA at best, and we know he knew the victim, so even that could've been explained; but what of the others? He had no known association with any of the other women that we could find, not a scrap of evidence puts him anywhere in their vicinity, either at the time the crimes were carried out, or at any other time."

"Come on stone; we all know you're supposed to have a superhuman brain or some shit, but you're wrong this time; this is our guy, I feel it in my gut." Thompson, one of my staunchest adversaries, was quick to shoot down my answer. Nothing new there, there was no love lost between us. He was a chauvinistic asshole, who'd thought it would be easy getting me into his bed, because apparently the women back in his hometown of bum fuck USA thought he was hot shit. I'd been brutally honest in my rejection, he hadn't been too appreciative of my candidness and has been a pain in my ass ever since.

I didn't let the slur bother me. Though it was a well-known tactic some used to throw people off their guard. I'm not that easily led and what others thought, didn't necessarily have the desired effect on me. That's probably why I'd gained the reputation of a stone cold bitch.

Whatever! Nothing deterred me from my purpose, nothing; not even the brief affair I'd had in college. When things had become too serious with Paul, and it had looked like I might be taken off track, I dropped the guy like a hot coal. That was my one and only foray into the shark infested waters called relationships. Somehow the other person always seemed to expect you to give up who you were, to please them.

With Paul, things had started out well enough. The physical side of things were ok, nothing earth shattering like I'd heard bragged about, but then he'd started to become controlling and wanting more and more of my time. Instead I'd given him his walking papers and severed all ties.

Some considered me heartless in the way I did things, the way I was so completely focused on getting ahead in my chosen field to the point that nothing else mattered in the least; that may be true. I do know a part of my heart died with my family that long ago day, and if I had to be a heartless loner to find the one who ended them, and brought this sorrow into my life,

then so be it. It has been my only
reason for living all these years later
and I won't quit until I found him.

I gathered my thoughts collectively, once more pulling everything in. Frank Connell was a little odd yes, with his quiet unassuming manner, the way he seemed to always be trying desperately to disappear into himself. I'm sure many people found this strange; but being strange did not make you a mass murderer. It just meant you were weary of your fellow man and knowing some of the shit I did, who could blame him?

"This is our guy." I pointed to the second screen, at the man who stood out for me. I knew there would be an outcry; my choice is an upstanding citizen. The CEO of a leading brokerage firm; everything about him looks great on paper, well his professional and public files anyway, but in interview I'd seen the taint on the shine.

Though he'd been there, not as a suspect, but as a character witness for his nephew, something about him had just jumped out at me. It wasn't anything I could put into words, as always with me, it came from a place beyond my control. That was partially problematic, because my superiors dealt in logistics and data. Two things I couldn't always readily provide with my theories, but thankfully my record has been stellar so far, so my decisions garnered me at least an unbiased look, instead of being shoved aside.

"You've got to be kidding me right, the uncle, seriously?"

"Yes, that's my guy." There was a lot of grumbling among the other occupants of the room, but I wouldn't back down just because no one else agreed. I didn't look to any of them for support, that's not my style. I'm a loner through and through and maybe that's why the bureau had decided to send me out alone on my first field assignment. Now was not the time to think about that though, for more reasons than one.

"Mind telling me how you arrived at that agent Stone?"

I looked at my boss the director, and took a deep breath. I might be gruff with everyone else, but this man held my future in his hands and I never forgot that. So even though I might think some of his decisions were crap, I still showed him the respect he was due.

Director Durant is a very no nonsense military type, in his late fifties early sixties. His salt and pepper hair was still worn shorn close to the scalp, as a throwback to his days in the army. His light blue eyes could be in turn compassionate and stern, and his gruff manner left no room for fuck ups. In all my dealings with him, I've always been reminded of the strict disciplinarian type, who would scold you bitterly one moment and feed you candy in the next.

"Okay, Frank just seems too obvious to me; like a red herring someone's dangling in our faces. Nothing was ever left behind at the first ten scenes. The news leaked that we were closing in on our doer and suddenly he decides to get sloppy and leave transferable DNA? I don't think so.

So I backtracked from there. Yes Frank knows this victim, but not in the way that would call for him to be leaving DNA on her body in the way it was found. So how did it get there? Obviously by someone who knew both the victim and the accused; in order to have that access, they had to be very close to both.

Now the rapes eliminate a female UnSub, so we're left with a male. Let's just say for the sake of argument, that it isn't the obvious Frank Connell, who decided to leave parts of himself all over his last victim, when he hasn't done it before. So who do we have that's a close male relative or friend, who could have access to his DNA, and also knew the victim?

We've already ascertained that Frank has no friends; he's a stay-at-home body, who hangs around with his elderly mother and putters around in the basement with his woodwork. Okay, so no male friends; as for relatives the only one we have is the uncle that's in state and has any kind of contact. So, with the elimination of friends and other family members due to time constraints, we're left with Samuel Connell." Short and precise.

"Come on director, you're not buying this are you? The guy's the CEO of a fortune 500 company." Thompson was, to say the least, furious with my assertions. He'd been on the same path for weeks now, as well as the others, who seemed okay with following along. Me, I'm not the following behind type. Yes I probably could've given them a heads up about my theory, but I wasn't here to hold their hands; and what would happen the next time when I wasn't there? How would they find the right thread on their own and pull?

"Who was brought up on charges of rape at the age of nineteen, while attending his Ivy League university; said charges were then dropped under very questionable circumstances." I informed him.

"What, where did you get that information?"

My colleagues scrambled to find the information in their files.

"You're not going to find it in there boys; I did the digging myself. You guys were so focused on Frank, you dropped the ball and left all the little extras untouched. I turned every stone and that's where I found Samuel Connell. Your CEO was also suspected of beating an ex-girlfriend almost to death, back in his early twenties. Again the charges were dropped under very obscure circumstances.

Over the years, there've been little bumps along the way, but he's had enough money and clout to keep them out of the public eye. And one last thing, Veronica Sharp, our last victim, told friends a couple weeks before her demise that she suspected him of criminal behavior. She never said what, but intimated that she was giving serious thought to contacting the authorities."

"We spoke to her neighbors and friends, no one told us this."

"It's all in the approach boys."

"You're full of crap, over a thousand man hours can't be wrong; you tell her director, there's no way this guy did those things."

Are you kidding me? This guy was seriously testing to become an agent, and this was his thought process? He sounded like a petulant two year old that didn't get his way, and was about to throw himself to the floor and have a tantrum. I held my tongue, because quite frankly, there was nothing to say. I'd given it my best and even with all my drive that's all I ever asked of myself.

"And you base your premise on what Agent Thompson?" The director, who had been studying us, finally broke his silence.

"He doesn't fit the profile; first of all he's at least twenty years older than the target age, he's an upstanding member of the community and he's married."

"So was the Green River killer."

Agent Thompson hung his head and threw up his hands in defeat. "I just don't see it, do any of you guys?"

Ross, Gervais and Kowalski kept their mouths shut and looked pensive; that's the way they've played it all throughout our time working this case, not wanting to stick their necks out lest they were wrong. Me, I gave it my best and my all and if at the end of the day I was wrong, then I sucked it up and combed through the case, until I came to the right conclusion. It was more important to me to get it right, than to get it fast, or first.

"So your argument agent Thompson, is that he doesn't fit the profile; well now that's why we're here isn't it? It's a new day, boys and girls, now we have to profile the profile. Let's not forget, there was a time in our history when it was believed that the shape of a man's head decided his guilt or innocence. We've come a long way since those green days, but we still have far yet to go." He exited his chair and with hands clasped behind his back, walked to the lone window overlooking the training fields.

"So what're you saying director?"

"I'm saying agent Thompson, that once again agent Stone has proven why she's our shining new star. Not only is she correct but her prognosis is spot on. What she did different to the rest of you, is look beneath the surface. She didn't just follow the textbook on this one; she used her skills of elimination, otherwise known as commonsense plain and simple. Good job agent Stone, now as for the rest of you, we have work to do." I got the official nod and without waiting around for the fallout, I gathered my things and exited the room. No doubt I will hear about this later as the fact that I hadn't shared my findings will be blamed for their failure, tough.

I'm glad that was over; that had been one of the toughest exercises so far, in spite of the crumbs that were placed in our way to direct us to our conclusion, which turns out was the wrong one. My fellow agents had proven how easy it is to accuse and convict the wrong person, based on our need to believe, that the more normal seeming, upstanding citizen, was always innocent; while the society reject, was always the guilty party.

The fact that Frank Connell is a fat, balding middle-aged recluse, painted him as guilty in their eyes. It was a sad fact that this kind of thinking had put many innocents behind bars, and worse yet, sent them to their deaths. I was willing to do everything I could to put a stop to such behaviors, one case at a time.

I left the building and headed to the cafeteria for some much-needed tea. Yes I know, what federal agent or law enforcement officer worth their salt preferred tea instead of coffee? I couldn't stomach the stuff; it tasted like lead paint in my mouth.

There was a lot of activity on the base this time of day. Cadets going through their rigorous paces, the echo of gunfire could be heard off in the distance, breaking that feeling of the serene one could sometimes get, when walking these grounds. Surrounded by hundreds of acres of wooded land, the Farm was a thing of beauty. It looked like any college campus in the country's Midwest, and in the fall, rivaled its neighbors in beauty.

I'd been here six months, instead of the usual four, because my case was a special one. I had been recruited into an accelerated special agent-training program, which meant hundreds of hours of training. It wasn't all physical training and firearms, though they too were essential. But I had to study all aspects of crime and law enforcement, which had been my field of study at the University. It had been a grueling few months, each day starting early and going on nonstop for twelve hours or sometimes more. I will miss it when I left, it was one of the only places that had felt like home in a very long time, I didn't want to know what that said about me.

Chapter 4

Mancini

My meet with Jason Laramie went smoothly; we finalized our dealings, no doubt under the watchful eye of law enforcement, from afar of course; which we had a good laugh over. The details of our little meeting, if revealed, could cause quite an uproar. Jace is one of my best friends, outside of my two brothers and my family; he got pretty much the same rap as I did, and it made us close.

In our line of work, trust was hard to come by, but we've known each other since we were young men. In fact, we'd become part of the same organization at about the same time, though Jace had beaten me to the punch by a few months. Another scion, from yet another wealthy family.

Our organization was kind of a secret society if you will, that the public had no knowledge of what so ever. It was best that it was kept that way, for all intents and purposes; though it made our lives a bit difficult. That was the price we paid for who we were, it gave us the freedom to move in the shadows, as we will. Had we applied our special skills to a law enforcement badge, we would've been more hindered than the criminals we sought to eradicate, which would've been not only a shame, but also a waste.

"So Hank, you all set for your meet with these guys later?"

"Yeah, that's set for another hour or so." I sat back in my chair, a little more relaxed now that the hard part was over. Planning for an Op was always grueling work, there was so much to cover, so much that could go wrong, and the consequences if we failed, which for me was never an option.

"Alright dude, I guess I'll leave so that you can get yourself together. I know how it is having to deal with them on an empty stomach; I don't begrudge you this part of the operation dude seriously. I think if I had to carry your load I would've burnt out by now."

"I doubt it Jace; we do this because we have to, because it needs to be done and most of all, because we don't trust anyone else to do it."

"This is true, and on that note, are you planning on settling down anytime soon brother?" We always ended our conversations the same.

"No bro I don't think so; I don't think that it'll be fair to anyone, you know what I mean? This lifestyle, she'd have to be one special woman." For some unknown reason, one Cierra Stone popped into my mind at that precise moment, but I brushed it aside.

I wasn't in the market for hearth and home, but something about her kept tugging at me, which was unacceptable. It was one thing to want to get her between the sheets, and quite another to start down that road of make believe. There was no room in my life for permanence, not now anyway, and maybe not ever. The little I'd garnered about her so far had rung true for me. It was almost as if she was my equal, that could be the reason for my fascination, I wasn't sure. I'll have to dig a little deeper into Ms. Stone's background at a later date.

"What about you, found anyone willing to put up with your shit yet?" If I was a hard ass, Jace was the poster boy. He was tough as nails, though his down home Louisiana, boy next door charm, could easily fool the unsuspecting into believing different.

"Nope not in the cards brother." He had a wistful look there for a moment, but it was too fleeting to be sure. Jace for all his tough outer shell, needed family. He'd lost his at a young age and was for all intents and purposes, pretty much alone in the world. That's why I shared mine with him; Juliet Mancini could melt even the iciest of hearts, and over the years, her gentle understanding had helped to mellow out my friend.

"So I'll get back to you after I meet with these guys and let you know the particulars, everything's pretty much set already though, unless they throw me a curve ball today, so we're a go."

"Can't wait to be done with this one, this one's left a really bad taste in my fucking mouth; these fucks are really sick. Sicker than the usual pricks we deal with and we've dealt with some sick shit before haven't we?" Jace stood to leave.

"I know what you mean brother, it takes all kinds; the fact that this bunch dresses up in suits and holds high positions in our society is what makes it so distasteful. But we knew going in that it wasn't always going to be the so called dregs of society that we were going to have to deal with; we knew going in that it was going to be some of the world's best sometimes that we'd have to bring down. Doesn't matter to me, guilty is guilty, I don't care if you're wearing a thousand dollar suit, or you're a fucking bum on the corner."

"I wonder that our government doesn't have the first clue that they're harboring these assholes, so much for national security, the shit is sickening."

"I know, that's why we're here, doesn't make it any easier though; so tell me before you go, how're you doing with the CIA, they still on your ass for that last run?"

"Brother please, they're always going to be in my shadow, doesn't phase me none; our boys have us covered, what about you?"

"I think I have a new shadow coming soon, I'm not sure about this one though."

"Yeah, why is that?"

"This one's a girl."

"Sheeiit they putting a female on you, what are they up to this time?"

"I don't know, have to wait and see. I'll keep you posted brother."

"You do that, keep your head down and your ass covered bro?"

"Will do, you do the same, drinks after?"

"You know it, how's my girl doing? I haven't spoken to her in a few days at least, been a bit busy trying to fine tune my part of the Op."

"Be forewarned, she's on the warpath again."

"Uh oh, what happened now?"

"Hell if I know, apparently we're not paying her enough attention. I know the spiel, she's working her way up to the get Hank married campaign." He laughed at that of course, because everyone knew how shamelessly relentless mama was in her drive to see me married off.

We said our goodbyes on a lighter note, granted that in a few days we'd both be in a much different place, facing danger, in our bid to free the world of scum, one criminal at a time.

After Jace left, I had a few minutes downtime before I had to be on the move again. Always before walking into one of these things I cleared my head, using an ancient technique an old master had taught me long ago. It called for total concentration and nothing more, just focus on releasing everything from my thoughts one at a time, until the mind and psyche were clear of all white noise.

Then replacing each parcel piece by piece. It was almost like washing the brain before restoring it with clean Intel. I couldn't afford to fuck up in this meeting, these guys had to buy what I was selling, hook line and sinker. Anything goes wrong and months of hard work goes down the drain. Though it was pretty much in the bag and things had already started moving, there was always that element of surprise. In this business, things changed from one moment to the next without warning, so it was never a good idea to take anything for granted.

Thoughts of Cierra flitted through my mind sporadically throughout the day, but each time I steadfastly banked them down; what was going on there was not something I could deal with right now, that was another minefield that had to be treaded carefully. One thing that had me just a little worried though, is the fact that she's already occupying so much of my thoughts and we hadn't even met as yet, what would meeting her in the flesh be like?

Jaxx had said she wasn't here yet and what little spying I'd had time to do hadn't shown exactly when she would be in my domain, but for some strange reason that escaped me, I felt strongly, that if she was watching me right now I would know. I didn't bother to study why I was so sure of that, I just sensed that I would be able to tell the difference if her eyes were on me.

When my business was done, and before she showed up on my doorstep, I'm going to have to sit down and analyze just what this all meant. This was no place for thoughts of the beauty though, not when I was about to meet with filth in a few hours, and that in and of itself was telling; I never gave a fuck before.

The Chinese delegates sat around the table as we discussed their next strategic move; the lying fuck interpreter rattled off his bullshit lies to me, while I bobbed my head like the shit he was saying made all the sense in the world. I listened in with my keen understanding of their language, as they gave orders to carry out their sadistic schemes, and it took everything in me not to jump up from my chair and chop all their fucking heads off.

Instead, I remained still with a look of unconcern on my face; these fucking demons were going to die, but not yet.

In all my years of doing this, the thing that I hated most out of all the evil that I came into contact with, was the harm to children; give me undeniable proof of an injustice done against a child, any child, and I will execute the perpetrator without a second thought; it was my only hard limit. Children are the innocents, to be protected and guarded against the darkness. What these fucks and others like them did to them was deserving of the harshest punishments imaginable.

The FBI and Interpol, along with some of the world's other leading investigative agencies have been hunting me for over a decade; they suspect me of criminal dealings, if they only knew, those fucks only wish they could do what I do. I've done more to eradicate evil in the relatively short time in my career, than they've all done collectively since their inception. That's because they're all headed by a den of serpents who has fooled the world for generations into believing that they're the protectors of mankind; that their only interest is in the betterment of the human condition; bullshit.

Corruption reached to the highest echelons of every major player in the field, money that great divider, made suckers out of the best of us. The leading law enforcement agencies were supposed to be protectors of our safety, people forgot that the men and women who headed said agencies were just human like them; prone to the same shortcomings as they were, just as capable of committing atrocities.

Put them in a position of power and worse yet, arm them, and you not only had a criminal on your hand, you had one who was now protected by bureaucracy and sanctioned by their host governments. I should know, I've dispatched enough of the scum to be aware that the evil that exists, reaches higher than the average person would even think to look. The thing was though, that you cut off one head and another grew back almost overnight, it's a vicious never-ending cycle.

The men I'm currently surrounded by today are under the misguided belief that I'm an expert in the trafficking of human flesh, along with many other sordid things. My portfolio, or at least the one serving this particular purpose, claims that I always get the job done: no losses, no repercussions. They were paying me millions to carry out their dirty work. Three million in fact, for the swift and undetected transport of ten teenaged Asian girls, who had been hand picked by a handful of wealthy elitist twisted fucks, who in turn, were willing to pay ten times that or more for the procurement of what would amount to sex slaves.

My part in that is the hardest, herding these girls together on a ship in China and hiding them through customs, until they disembarked off the shores of America. Then if all goes well according to their agenda, one of their henchmen will take possession of the merchandise and be in the wind, the young victims never to be seen or heard from again, at least not by anyone from their past.

This particular run has been in the works for two months; believe it or not, the selling of human beings is easier than the world has been led to believe; the acquiring of human flesh for all manner of despicable services is big business. It's my estimation, that some men and women, once they've amassed astronomical sums of money, lose their fucking minds and anything resembling a conscience. These beings then become so bored, that they throw each other little secret parties where they concoct some of the sickest shit your mind could ever imagine and then some.

This scheme is the brainchild of one such demon; he somehow convinced nine of his cohorts that this was the next best thing to do. These highly esteemed douche bags, some of whom were even now joking about the demise of these children, has made this into an art form.

By day they're the supposed law-abiding, upstanding citizens representing their respective nations on foreign soil; by night they're every child's worst nightmare.

Both factions were led by one common denominator, money; one had too much and so turned to using it for evil purposes, while the other for their own love and greed of it, were willing to do anything up to and including selling their souls to attain it. The delegates saw nothing wrong with selling their countrymen and women into all manner of horrific situations, their consciences were clear, because these particular children were from families of lower class, and hey, the place was over populated anyway right? Fucking assholes.

"So we're set gentlemen yeah?" I needed to get the fuck out of there quick, before I said fuck it and offed every last man in the room, couldn't rush my hand, their time will come.

"You will let us know how everything goes with the merchandise immediately yes, our clients are very anxious to accept delivery."

Yeah and then I'll snap your fucking neck you pig

Chapter 5

Cierra

"Cierra Stone, paging Cierra Stone."

"Shit Gracie! What can that be about now?" I put the brush down and turned to my roommate.

"You won't know until you go see."

"I hope there isn't anything more for me to study, this guy is like a freaking shadow as it is. I don't know why they think I'll be any help, since they haven't been able to nail him in the last ten years or so, and I'm not sure why they need a profiler on this one, hasn't he been profiled to death?"

"Girl kill that noise, you know you have mad skills beyond profiling, otherwise they'd never have tapped you for the job, besides, that piece of eye candy is the best subject they've got going in the bureau these days, yum." She twitched her eyebrows at me in her comical way.

"How can you tell? Every picture's a profile shot, it's almost as if he knows where the cameras are and keeps his face in the shadows."

"Well, I heard from this girl that was in one of my classes that he's fuck hot and rumor has it that he's hung like a gorilla." She was all but drooling now.

"I think gorillas are supposed to have small dicks." I think I saw that on the discovery channel, but I couldn't be sure.

"You know what I mean."

"Gracie, you do know I'm supposed to be gathering info to put this guy away for a long, long time right? Not trying to jump him."

"Nothing wrong with enjoying the scenery while you're at it now is there?"

Gracie was the least likely candidate for the Academy. A brash, loud talking, always ready to throw down as she terms it, African American beauty, with chocolate brown skin and the most piercing black eyes with the purest whites. She looked about fifteen, except for her height of five ten, which towered over my five three stature. From our first day together at the Academy, we'd just hit it off. Our backgrounds weren't much different; Gracie grew up about an hour or so away in D.C.'s inner city.

Tough streets for anyone, but even more so for a young girl who's father had been gunned down for his part in a neighborhood watch. She'd had to stay in that environment her whole life, until her quick brain and aptitude for science got her out.

Now she was thought to be someone to watch in the field of forensic science. Though we'd mentioned our families and what had happened to them, we'd never actually come out and said that it was because of these incidents that we had fought so hard to get where we are. I sometimes wondered if we had the same agenda; though her father's murderer had been caught and tried, there'd always been speculation that there was more involved and that all the players had not been brought to justice.

"I've got to go, Durant isn't known for his patience."

"Lucky duck, I bet they're calling to send you on your way; oh New York and the great Hank Mancini."

"I can only hope, I've been studying this guy so long now it's like I know his every move."

"Don't get too cocky, I bet everyone who's gone after him felt the same way in the beginning."

"I've learned from their mistakes, I won't be making the same." I left the dorm like room that I'd been sharing with the other woman for the past six months. I'd fast tracked it through Quantico ever since they'd snatched me up my senior year at Vassar. It was a dream job for me, something I'd worked towards my whole life, ever since a mad man had killed my parents and my younger brother when I was eight.

My dream of becoming a ballerina had died a fiery death on a little hill in Maryland. On that day, something had been born in me, a thirst for vengeance. The need to bring criminals to justice; it had become my passion. I'd spent everyday since then, with a few exceptions, focused on achieving that goal and nothing was going to stand in the way.

In school I'd flung my way through my classes; always at the top. Scholarships had helped a poor orphan from the worst part of Baltimore's inner city make it into one of the nation's leading schools, from where I'd caught the notice of the Bureau; just where I wanted to be. The animal that had slaughtered my family had never been caught and I will never rest until that day came. If I had to babysit a master criminal like Hank Mancini in the meantime, then whatever it takes; there's nothing stopping me from working on both things at the same time.

"You wanted to see me director?"

"Come in, sit down."

Well hello to you too; my superior was to say the least...abrasive. He's a gruff no nonsense type who never smiles and rarely laughs, at least not that I've noticed; and although he'd offered praise when I did well in my exercises, like the Connell case a few days ago, this was his usual way. He could praise you with one breath and tear you apart with the next. His nickname around the bureau is chuckles, which no one would ever dare call him to his face. Whatever the case, he's been director for almost twenty-five years, one of the longest terms in the history of the bureau.

I took my seat in one of the visitor's chairs across from his desk, folded my arms and crossed my legs. His office was very much like his personality, Spartan; neat and everything in its place, there wasn't so much as a paper clip out of place. Pictures of his wife, kids and grandkids graced the top of his huge high glossed mahogany desk. The wall behind him was covered with varying certificates of his achievements, as well as awards for his service to his country.

"You leave tomorrow morning at seven, that'll put you in New York at about roughly ten o'clock. An agent Peter Sarkozy will be there to meet you and debrief you on the subject's latest movements. You've been given his portfolio and should've already studied him and become very well acquainted with the way he works. Hank Mancini is an enigma; no one knows the real man and we barely understand his public persona. He comes from one of the wealthiest families in the country, went to the best schools and had the opportunity to be anything he wanted to be in this life; he chose instead to be a criminal.

In almost ten years we've not been able to pin any one thing on him, but where there's smoke there's usually fire and he's surrounded by a lot of smoke."

Or the smoke could just be vapor. Of course I didn't say that out loud, I didn't want to commit professional suicide after all, but the truth is, I've studied all the info I'd been given and something just didn't ring true. Hank Mancini had been an exceptional student his whole scholastic career, until his nineteenth year. He'd been an upstanding citizen for all intents and purposes, then for some unfathomable reason, he'd simply dropped off the face of the earth not to be heard from again, until six years later at the age of twenty-five. Now almost nine years later he was still evading law enforcement and on the rare occasion that he was actually brought in, he just slipped through somehow without so much as a blemish on his record.

He's been on the FBI's most wanted list in the top billing for eight years running, and now the job has fallen to me since so many others before me have failed, to find out the truth about the man and bring him down, bring him to justice if need be. No one seemed in doubt of his guilt, his movements were just too suspect according to law enforcement, it was not very well known in the bureau how he first came to be on our radar, that hadn't been in any of the research I'd done, which in itself was a mystery, but my job was not to question my superiors no matter how much I might want to know.

The problem is, I'm not so sure of what I was looking for, it had all been done already as far as I could tell. Each time we got a whiff of something to do with the great Mancini, we sent someone out, and each time they came back with their tales between their legs, or their ass handed to them.

Not only that, but the guy was a career ender. Quite a few of my colleagues had lost their jobs or positions after tussling with this guy, and I knew what my superiors expected of me as the only female to ever go up against this mastermind; they didn't just want me to use my mind, I was pretty sure they wanted me to use a lot more than that if push came to shove; that's how desperate they'd become.

Mancini

I needed a little downtime to get the stench of the last few days off of me, so I decided to relax by taking my boat out on the water for a little spin. One of my pleasures, sailing, in fact I like anything to do with leisure, yachting, racing boats, cars and bikes; I even enjoyed a little rock climbing every once in a while. Those things kept me sharp, because they involved staying very focused in order to avoid danger.

Today, with the business of filth out of the way, my mind turned to more pleasant enticements; like the eyes of one Cierra Stone. I felt the tightening pull in my gut at the memory of what she looked like; on my desk at home in my personal office I had a glossary that I'd already collected since learning of her existence. By the time the beauty came into my atmosphere I will know her inside and out, as much I'm sure as she probably believes she knows me.

For some strange reason I found that I was reluctant to dig into her past at this particular time, not while I was dealing with the scum of the earth, and that in itself was very telling as well, since when did I care about such menial things? I was beginning to get just a little worried about the strange hold she seemed to have on me; it was her eyes, those amazing sky blue orbs had seemed to look right through me. If I weren't careful, she'd have me falling at her feet before she even landed, and that couldn't be allowed. The lady was coming here to study me, in order to put me away for a long long time after all, only a fool would be interested in getting burnt like that.

There was nothing for it though, I'd seen and I'd wanted, and what Hank Mancini wanted, he usually took.

Too bad we'll have to do the waltz before I can take her to bed, but make no mistake about it, she will be gracing my bed before long.

The next day was spent at home locked away behind closed doors going over everything I needed to do in order for my latest operation to go off without a hitch, I couldn't pay too much attention to the feds and whoever else were on me this week I had innocents depending on me and nothing was going to stand in the way of that. They never knew where I was or what I was doing always in my dust which I'm sure was a bone of contention for them, I wasn't too torn up about it though, I hated them as much as they hated me.

Having law enforcement on your ass twenty four seven wasn't very fun though so I'd devised ways of out maneuvering them for the past six or seven years, now they were hard pressed to even catch an occasional glimpse of me unless I wanted to fuck with them just for kicks which couldn't be easy for their jobs, how the hell could you watch someone you couldn't see? But still they persisted.

That night I went to one of my clubs to unwind; it was my night to see and be seen I guess you could say and not even the entertainment up on stage kept eyes off of me. This was my favorite place I bought it as an escape from my daily life and I've made sure this place stayed free of all that other bullshit that usually played out in night clubs; no drugs no strippers no under the table dealings of any kind.

I paid my guys top dollar to see that things stayed that way. The liquor was top shelf all the way the food above par and entertainment was always top billing. Tonight's band was a red-hot European techno group whose latest CD had gone platinum; they cost a mint but the door charge alone will more than pay for it.

There were private booths for the more upscale clientele who preferred privacy along with their entertainment; no sexual activities allowed though. The V.I.P. rooms are always occupied by some socialite or diplomatic businessman; or someone who had the money to afford the hourly rate. I come from money so I understand better than most that money brings money; people of wealth would rather spend money with their own kind that's why you have society mavens chairing charities instead of the poor housewife who actually knows what the fuck she's talking about.

I was on my second snifter of Louis XIV cognac when she walked in it's a good thing I was sitting alone because my reaction was very unHank like. She fucking caught me off guard; in her official photo you can see the potential for beauty with her tightly pulled back hair, face bare of enhancements she looked about eighteen there; beautiful yes, but you couldn't get the full effect, the woman standing before me was no hidden beauty she was fucking gorgeous.

All that jet-black hair down around her shoulders with those blue blue eyes in a face molded and sculpted to perfection. At least that's what she looked like to me as she stood there. Two things went through my head at once, my heart had kicked, I'll have to examine that later, and my dick took notice, something that hasn't happened in too long to remember. I'd become so jaded that sex was just something you did to scratch an itch. Something told me things were going to be way different this time.

Her body in the low riding jeans that molded slender hips and the tight top that showed off just a hint of cleavage was spectacular, someone had done their homework, I didn't go for the overly made-up ass hanging out type. They'd sent me the perfect package, I hope for her sake they knew what the fuck they were doing.

She looked as though she was on the prowl and I knew just who her prey was; I noticed others noticing her as well and my ire rose just a little. Back the fuck off boys, this one's mine no sense in fighting that persistent feeling in my gut who knows where it would all lead? But I was willing to find out.

After my initial jolt when my body had literally started I played it cool; eyes half lidded I swirled my snifter around as I pretended not to notice her casing the room. I felt the moment her gaze landed on me it was almost like an electrical charge, like touching a live wire. I caught the slight flush and her faltering step from beneath my lashes as well.

Game on.

Cierra

The music sounded like something out of a fast paced movie; one of those race car things with ex-cons always coming out on top; how fitting. I hadn't wanted to make my debut in this way and in this place, Hank Mancini's reportedly favorite nightclub. I'm essentially on his turf but word on the street is that he has a job in the works and we needed to move fast. I'd barely landed in the city before I was being put out to pasture.

Agent Sarkozy had met me at the airport as prearranged and literally went right to it. He was rattling off Intel before we reached baggage claims. " Our boy has something in the works lots of movement in the last couple days. He also met with Jason Laramie another known criminal who always seems to stay one step ahead of us but we feel pretty positive about this one." He seemed overly excited and just a tad hyper active he also talked as fast as he walked.

"In the last two days or so Mancini has been seen making the rounds so to speak, this guy never goes into the same place twice at least not within the same time frame so it's hard really keeping track of who what where and why. As you know we're no longer allowed by law to plant listening devices or any other kind for that matter in any of his places. The obvious answer to that would've been to hit his local hangouts but the thing is he only hangs out in his places."

"We don't know as yet who he's been meeting with except for Laramie but we feel pretty certain there's something brewing we only get this much action out of him when he has a job lined up, otherwise believe it or not the guy's kind of a home body. We haven't seen the girlfriend lately either and I use the term lightly because Mancini as far as we can tell don't have girlfriends in as much as he has bed partners. He does seem to be monogamous though. So any questions?"

I guess he was finally ready to wind down. "I can't think of any right this minute no, I've studied everything we have on him so far, have sort of a handle on the ins and outs but what I'm not really sure about is why we need a profiler on this one."

"Well I'm sure you understand you're more than a profiler on this one, I mean yeah you need to get in there and see what makes this guy tick, but so far everyone we've put on him have come up empty, this time we're hoping to do things a little different, we're hoping by sending in a female it would make a difference. An attractive female with your skills is like killing two birds with one stone, plus from what I hear you have something unique going on along with your profiling or at least that's what the boys upstairs seem to think."

That was kind of news to me but I didn't let on in anyway as we headed out of the terminal into the busy parking lot. I'd been so caught up in his words I hadn't even noticed much of anything around me. It was busy as was to be expected in any major city airport with people coming and going by the dozens even at this early hour in the morning.

The black nondescript sedan, which is de rigueur for the bureau was a cool welcome after the early morning heat.

"So you ready Agent Stone?"

"Of course, when do I meet the rest of our team?"

"Um you will get to meet the others in a day or so right now we have to get moving, sorry but there won't be a grace period I'm afraid we'll be sending you in and soon as you land."

"What now?" I looked down at the linen travelling shorts I wore with the silk top that would no doubt be wilted in the next hour in this oppressive heat as he laughed.

"Not right this minute no, but you will be going to his place tonight, like I said we think he's got something going and though there's no pattern that we can follow because he's extremely sly and his movements are never uniform we do hope he'll show up there tonight. If not we'll just have to try again tomorrow night, whatever it takes to get you two in the same place at the same time."

We spent the rest of the ride into lower Manhattan going over every minute detail as I found that I did have some questions after all. Agent Sarkozy was very forthcoming and I didn't get the resentment vibe I'd lived with on the Farm. By the time he dropped me off at what would be my new place of residence for the next little while, I felt confident that I could do what I came here for, bring down the great Mancini.

Chapter 6

Cierra

It's a good thing the bureau had shelled out the money for my clothes as well as a stylist as it was a sad fact that I was sorely lacking in this department. Not that I'm a complete and total lost but I always had something of more importance to do than worrying about what I was wearing or how my hair looked. The basic grooming has always worked just fine for me but I understood the need for the extra help they'd provided.

I spent the afternoon relaxing as much as one could relax when about to beard the lion in his den, I went over everything again to the point I could recite it verbatim. I remembered

Gracie's words about being too cocky and took them to heart, it was true I'd heard the stories of others before me who had thought they would be the one to stop the man in his tracks and every last one of them to a man had failed, some of them worst than others. I had no intentions on failing though, one way or the other I was going to get to the bottom of this Mancini curse at it had come to be known.

The club was one of those high-end type deals with chrome, glass and marble everywhere. The seating looked like blue velvet but on closer inspection was actually suede. There was gold -framed beveled glass on all the walls throughout; the platform stage was huge and they were three bars on the first level alone that I could see. I'd asked if it wouldn't have been better to have a partner with me here tonight but my handlers decided that since my purpose was catching Hank's eye it would be better played to fly solo.

For some reason I'm extremely nervous all of a sudden, some of my earlier confidence having abated. Thank heaven they didn't make me wear something short and sluttastic or I would really be out of my element. The slim fitting jeans were as far out of my comfort zone as I was willing to go; paired with the V-neck top that bordered on the risqué and the three inch heeled fuck me shoes I guess I fit in perfectly with this crowd.

My first sight of him in the flesh was...okay, I'm a federal agent and we're bad ass professionals but the truth of the matter is that my first look at the elusive criminal was awe-inspiring. There I've admitted it to myself, that black wild windblown hair paired with those piercing blue green eyes were damn near lethal together. It didn't help that he had kick ass dimples that were evident even without a smile. I had to play it off like I wasn't here solely to spy on him so I let my gaze just glance off of him but boy did I want to take a second look and how unprofessional was that? You're here to catch a criminal Cierra not moon over him like an impressionable teenage girl.

I'd barely got enough of a glimpse of broad shoulders in a black V-neck black label with just a speck of white from the undershirt; his hand played with the glass he held between long tapered fingers. No doubt manicured to a high-gloss because for all his criminal mien the guy seemed to like his prissy comforts. Manicures every Tuesday, I'm a female and even I didn't have time to get that done as often as I'd like. I knew his itinerary by heart; aside from the mani-pedis he had a standing appointment every Thursday with one of the top stylists in the city to get his hair done.

He bought all his designer suits, well the ones he bought in New York at least from the same high-end menswear design store heavy on the Armani and Gucci. He owns homes in almost every major city here and in Europe or his family does at least and those were only the ones we knew of. It was thought that his net worth was well above a hundred billion and counting; that's way too much money for someone so young to have it just made him a target for all kinds of innuendo and speculation.

Like the bureau, they were so sure that he was up to his eyeballs in criminal activities even without a shred of evidence to support their claims and that was due mostly in part to his amassing of such great wealth without anyone knowing how. After all these years they still held fast to their instincts though proof or no proof. The guy has gone through some of the best we had to offer without seemingly missing a step, always coming out on top; that kind of luck had to run out sometime.

That's where I come in unlike the others before me who've failed I didn't plan to join that particular rank, if there was something there I would find it. I have to this is my first real assignment after all I couldn't afford to lose. It didn't even bother me too much that my superiors had thrown me into shark-infested waters my first time out I couldn't wait to prove my mettle. The puzzling and just a little confusing thing is I'm still not sure how to go about bringing down the bastard.

"Good evening Miss will there be just the one this evening?" A gorgeous young blonde approached me with a wide smile bringing me back to the present.

"Oh yes I'd prefer something a little farther away from the action if you don't mind."

"No problem this way please." She led me to a corner booth where I could still see the stage but was far enough away not to be caught in the heavy traffic and bonus I was now seated only two tables down from my target.

"Your server will be right with you enjoy your evening."

"Thank you." I'm not exactly comfortable in this sort of environment but my time in the Academy had taught me how to assimilate into any and all situations so I placed my little clutch purse on the table and folded my arms looking for all the world like a bored trust fund baby. My piece was on my ankle but I still felt almost naked with just the one it'll have to do though because there was nowhere to put the other in this getup. Although I'm more of a brain than brawn agent I'm very proficient with weapons and liked feeling the weight of a gun in my bag especially when in enemy territory; though there had never been any reports of Mancini becoming violent, no Mr. Smooth was way too cool for that, he just annihilated his enemies in a whole other and might I add effective way.

I figured enough time had passed that if I took another look it wouldn't seem too obvious but what I wasn't expecting when I turned in his direction was to connect with those jewel toned eyes watching me head-on. Shit they were even more spectacular this close I couldn't imagine what it would be like to look into those babies up close and personal: probably go into shock. He bowed his head slightly in acknowledgement that sexy glare penetrating right through to the core of me, making me feel just a little more out of my element. You better get it together girl this was no time to be lax, but it was like falling into a predator's eyes. I'll have to remember to tell Gracie that she was right about the eye candy bit.

I inclined my head slightly but withheld my smile couldn't play too easy now could I? A man like that might grow suspicious if I did that then again he's probably accustomed to strange women coming on to him, I wouldn't doubt it, the pictures the bureau had of him didn't even come close.

He lifted his snifter in salute and took a sip, which for some strange reason made me blush; a young nubile thing, which now come to think of it seemed to be the only type working here, came over to take my drink order. I so wanted a milkshake right now. I almost laughed at the thought, yeah that'll look really sophisticated Cierra granted they even served those things in a place like this.

"Do you happen to carry Riesling or maybe a pink Moscato?"

"Yes ma'am we have both this evening what's your preference?"

"I'll go with the Riesling thank you." Have to stick to sweet wines I hate the taste of wine but at least the sweet ones were somewhat palatable. I don't know what the hell is up with the wealthy and their screwball tastes; they enjoyed some of the strangest things, like snails, who the hell ever came up with that idea? Okay Cierra dude put the whammy on you with those orbs or something because you're not exactly thinking like a federal agent right now. In fact you haven't given the job much thought since you got here have you?

Awkward, I have nothing to do with my hands while I wait for my drink, I couldn't very well stare at him and I didn't want to look around like I was casing the joint which is exactly what I'm doing in essence. It was strongly believed by the bureau that this place is clean; there was nothing picked up the one time the Feds had been successful in planting bugs throughout all of Mancini's establishments then again it only lasted a few days before they'd been detected and removed.

Ever since then Hank has been overly vigilant when it came to his businesses, his homes and his offices even his vehicles were swept often apparently. We haven't been able to bug him in years plus with the new Federal laws it wasn't as easy to get warrants to plant listening and spying devices on citizens without solid proof that they were involved in some kind of threatening crime.

Everyone knows there was nothing on this guy, every time he came up against law enforcement and won it was bandied about on the front pages and on television; needless to say the public loved him; he was their hero for defeating 'the man' time and again and it didn't matter that he was a multi billionaire the poor of this city thought he did everything but walked on water because of his generosity. I didn't care if he gave every dime to the needy if he's guilty I'm going to be the one to bring him down I'm sure of it, it didn't matter that he made my stomach tremble

Chapter 7

Mancini

Poor thing she's so out of her element; I'd read her file, knew all about her background her education, her friends so I knew this wasn't the type of place she frequented, from what little I'd gathered so far Ms. Stone was a little bit of a recluse, something we both had in common. I know about the one short-lived affair she'd had in college, the way that had ended but not necessarily the why; I probably knew more about her than the bureau had on me.

I was tempted to approach her first but then I thought nah, let her work for it. She had no idea that I knew who she was and I couldn't wait to see how she handled her approach. I know the deal is for me not to know who she is like some sort of Mata Hari I guess but they knew I wouldn't be that easy so I wondered what angle they'd decided to use to draw me in.

I had to admit that for all my sordid dealings with the opposite sex she had something new, I'm not sure if it was her air of innocence that she tried so hard to hide or that natural sensuality that exuded from her. For all I know it could be just the mere fact that she was the first female the bureau had sent into the game the first agent they've tried to get this close.

The fact that she was fucking stunning didn't hurt either. I'd originally planned to play with her, a little game of cat and mouse but now I'm not so sure; this one might take something out of me that I'm not sure I was ready to give, I wasn't exactly comfortable with the things she made me feel truth be known, I liked being in control at all times, somehow the lady made me feel less in control of my own feelings, something I've been able to master for a very long time; then again when have I ever backed down from a challenge?

Cierra

With drink in hand I tried to play the sophisticate looking around sparingly as though I was people watching; why wasn't he making a move yet? Am I such a dog that even a notorious skirt chaser like him wouldn't take the bait? That was a very unsettling thought I mean job or not I'm still a female with all the feminine wiles. I felt heat rise in my cheeks at my own thoughts, maybe in retrospect it had been a bit presumptuous to think that he'd take one look and fall all over himself trying to get to me.

I guess I'll have to go with the fallback plan, if he doesn't approach me I'm supposed to manufacture a reason for approaching him. We'd already worked out a scenario and again I'm eternally grateful that seduction wasn't the first item on the menu though it was indeed on the list. When the waitress came back around I put my plan into action no sense in wasting time.

"So I'm new to the city and a friend recommended this place I'm very interested in possibly having some kind of promotional type thing here and I was wondering if the owner might be around?"

"Well maybe I can get you a manager...."

"No no no I prefer dealing with owners as opposed to management when talking these kind of numbers you understand!"

"Sure let me see what I can do ma'am." She took my order for another glass of wine before turning away; I watched her from the corner of my eye as she approached him and saw when the bastard shook his head and handed her his card to give to me.

Son of a ...She returned with my drink and the proffered card.

" I spoke with Mr. Mancini who happens to be here tonight and he said I should pass on his business card since he prefers not to handle any business dealings this evening; but if you'd like you can call him between eight and five tomorrow." I think she smirked at me when she said that and I felt my ire rise; how dare he try to brush me off as if I were nothing? He hadn't even bothered to look at me when he did it the bastard.

I swear I'm going to make him pay for that slight. And on that note you need to calm down girlie, what the hell happened to you? You're acting like a jilted lover and not at all like the special agent who has been assigned to bring down a master criminal. If just one look at the man in the flesh was going to cause this much turmoil this was going to be an uphill battle. You need to calm down and start thinking like the federal agent that landed in

New York this morning and not some lovesick teenybopper. That little pep talk helped to smooth my ruffled feathers just barely and I sat back in my chair as I thought of my next move, what I really wanted to do was march over there and give him a piece of my mind, insufferable jerk.

Mancini

Ball's back in your court Cierra now what are you going to do? There was only one thing left for her to do she'd already played her hand so she couldn't back down now, either she'd wait until tomorrow which I was pretty sure she wouldn't do or she'd find her way to me before the night was over under this made-up guise.

I could practically feel her pique from across the room she didn't like being thwarted but too bad; if she thought I was going to be easy prey then she really hadn't done her homework very well. I'm almost certain she did though because the bureau knew better than to send an inferior after me; each time I'd sent one of theirs back to them with his ass handed to him they'd brought out the big guns. I think I've been through all their best in the last eight years or so.

There was one glaring problem now though; I've never wanted to fuck my antagonist before. And is that all you want Hank? I ignored the annoying little voice in my head for now, whatever was going on here was going to have to wait until our business was done, until she was no longer hunting me, I hoped I could hold out for that long, something told me I was about to meet my match in more ways than one.

Here we go I guess she's decided to make her play; let's see how well she played the game, it could mean the difference in how things played out between us in the personal arena. I hope I wasn't going to have to be too hard on her; I'll just have to curtail my natural propensity for destroying anything to do with law enforcement.

"Good evening Mr. Mancini, mind if I have word?"

"Sure have a seat."

Magnificent, up close she was a natural beauty what could be mistaken for artificial enhancements from afar is actually the beauty of unblemished skin with nothing more than moisturizer I'm guessing. I let my eyes feed on her boldly, after all she was a beautiful woman she might find it strange if a player like I've been rumored to be didn't show at least a minute interest. She took the chair across from me and folded her arms on the table in front of her. "So, what can I do for you Miss....?"

"Stone, Cierra Stone."

"A name as beautiful as its owner; so tell me Miss Cierra Stone to what do I owe the pleasure of your company?"

"I'm not sure if your employee explained my needs to you..."

"She did; and I explained to her that I'm not interested in discussing business at this time however..."

"Yes I heard, tomorrow is better for you tell me Hank, I may call you Hank yes?"

I inclined my head and hid my smile; the little cat was showing her claws already she really didn't like being put off.

"As I was about to say do you always disregard such lucrative business deals? If so then I don't see how you've amassed your reputed wealth with such lax business practices."

"Is that right? Okay Ms. Stone you've peaked my interest exactly what did you have in mind?"

I could see that threw her since she wasn't expecting me to capitulate that easily. It was easy to since I had no plans on letting this farce go much farther but it was nice putting her through her paces.

"I'm interested in renting out your space maybe having a private party for a hundred people or so."

I looked at her for a minute before answering, let her sweat.

"Sorry not interested."

"Pardon?"

Oh that ruffled your feathers did it sweetheart?

"It wouldn't be cost-effective for me to do that; I make more money in one hour than I would by renting you the space for such a small number, unless you were willing to pay the premium plus overhead, plus the fee per person not to mention the liquor charge. So you see your little venture really doesn't hold any appeal for me."

Chew on that agent Stone let's see what else you have in that bag of tricks of yours, her eyes smoldered for just a second before she got it under control.

Fuck, I think the boys in Virginia had finally come up with something worthwhile, who knew they could attract such beauty? The fact that my dick was paying attention didn't sway me though I'm going to make her work for every tidbit she took back to them.

Chapter 8

Cierra

I think he's toying with me. It's the only explanation I could come up with. But why? There's no way he can know my true purpose and yet I can't quite put my finger on it but I know he's playing me. It would be really embarrassing to go back to my superiors with my ass handed to me so soon. I see now how he's always outmaneuvered the others that came before me; he's a smooth one Hank Mancini, his trick; never want what the other guy was selling.

Okay, I made my play and got rebuffed but this is just the beginning and though I prefer to go a different route, it looks like I'll have to use the old clichéd strategy though he didn't exactly bite. I felt my face heat up at the thought and refused to let myself go down that road of self- castigation again. I'd always been more focused on my career choice than my social life so I had never really had time to notice what men thought of me.

My one short lived affair had been pretty tame according to some of the stories I'd heard around campus, or maybe it was just me, maybe I'd been so focused on my goal of vengeance all my life that I hadn't taken time to notice anything else, like what kind of effect I had on the opposite sex. I know one thing it was so not a good feeling getting shot down by a known player.

"Well I guess that's that then Mr. Mancini thanks for your time."

I got up to return to my table, it felt like the walk of shame for some reason but I kept my head up and my shoulders squared thinking all the while what my next move should be. I had no intention on giving up but the elusive Mr. Mancini had no way of knowing that.

"Ms. Stone!"

Gotcha!

I erased the sudden smile from my face before turning around to face him again.

"Yes?"

"Why don't you join me for the rest of the evening since it appears we're both flying solo? Sit, relax what are you drinking? Let me get you a new glass."

I returned to my seat across from him and sat gingerly; my heart started racing now when it hadn't before at least not like this. That other felt like work, it was easy, simple; somehow this felt more personal like I was meeting him on a more intimate level. He'd shot down my offer but now had opened up the playing field again and somehow it felt different with him being the one to instigate my return, more personal.

"So what's your poison Cierra?"

"Riesling please."

He raised his hand and beckoned someone behind me; the same waitress from before came over to take our orders and she wasn't smirking this time. It looked more like she'd swallowed a lemon.

"What can I get you sir?"

"Get the lady her Riesling and bring us the Mediterranean platter please."

How very cordial and professional I wonder if he knew she wanted to jump his bones? And why should that thought bother you? You aren't interested in the slightest remember?

Mancini

"So Cierra Stone tell me about yourself."

"What would you like to know Mr. Mancini?"

Did she have any idea of the danger she was in right now with that flirty look she was throwing my way? I wondered how much of that was real and how much was her job because I had no doubt that she was attracted as I was but she was a cool one; not by so much as a twinge did she give away any sign of discomfort at this new turn of events, in fact other than the slight color in her cheeks there was nothing to give her away; well done agent Stone.

I'd read her profile from front to back so I knew this was her first real field operation; so far she'd been tested in controlled situations but this little gander was her first foray into the real world; too bad she was going to fail.

"What would you like to tell me Cierra?" Like a cat with a trapped mouse; the imagined visual almost made me smile.

"That's a weird way to put it what if I wished to remain a mystery? After all there's an allure in that isn't there?"

"For some yes but I prefer my relationships to be upfront and open I'm not so big on secrets." Make of that little tidbit what you will special agent; she made a slight shift on her seat before settling herself again, had I not been watching so closely I would've missed it. Good to know she wasn't exactly comfortable with the deception. I'm still going to make her pay for it though before I fuck her to within an inch of her life.

"I'm not sure I'm comfortable discussing myself with you on such short acquaintance after all what do I really know about you?"

"This is true; so what would you like to know? Ask me anything."

"Well I didn't exactly come prepared with a list of personal questions this might take some thought."

Liar! You know down to the last question mark what you want to ask me; I bet you've dreamt about it every night since my name and file came across your desk. I didn't utter a word of my inner thoughts just smiled innocently and watched her, it was hard not to; she had this one lock of hair that kept falling forward into her face every time she moved and my fingers itched to touch. Her lips were wide and sexy as fuck conjuring up all manner of illicit activities in my mind. They were painted a natural shade that did not distract from their sensuality but enhanced. I wonder what she'd do if she knew just what I was thinking of doing to her? What I absolutely planned on doing to her in the not too distant future. I brought my thoughts back to the conversation at hand putting aside my more lascivious thoughts for later.

"Okay then I'll start I'll tell you something personal about myself then you tell me something about you, sounds good?"

She shrugged her shoulders and fiddled with her glass; I'm sure she knew it wouldn't be that easy to garner information from me and I had no intentions of making her job anything less than difficult but I did plan on having lots of fun with her in the meantime.

"I'm extremely attracted to you." There it goes again that little telltale sign that I was getting to her, it showed in the quick inhalation of breath and the pulse in her neck that went suddenly into overdrive.

"That's rather blunt don't you think?"

"Like I said I treasure honesty and straightforwardness in others so how can I give less of myself? That blush is very becoming by the way and very rare if not refreshing." It's going to be a joy to explore just how deep that innocence ran; I can't wait to feel the heat of that blush under my tongue.

"Well thank you for the compliment but I'm sure you've said that to plenty of women before."

"Not those exact words no, may I speak frankly?"

"I thought you already were." She smiled a little uneasily at me.

"I like women, some more than others; I like the way they look, smell, taste but I don't fuck every woman I like and I don't necessarily like everywoman I fuck, you I'd love to fuck."

"Are you trying to shock me or is this your usual style? And if it is let me just say it leaves much to be desired."

There's that fire; you want to spit in my eye don't you beauty? No worries by the time we're through with each other you'll be begging me to mount you. I guarantee it.

"So you don't like the direct approach; I take it you prefer the game playing, beating around the bush, doing the dance?"

"I prefer not to be treated like an object..."

"I would think being told you're highly desirable would be taken as a complement."

"But that's not quite what you said now is it?"

"I thought it was I just said it in a more upfront way, my intentions are

on the table so there's no guessing
involved you know exactly where I
want this little encounter to go it's up
to you if you bite or not." Hopefully
the day will come when she'd forgive
me for treating her so crassly but I
have to admit to being just a little
pissed that she was sitting across from
me dreaming up ways to trap me.

Cat and mouse games aside, what she was doing was deceitful job or not; at least that's how I see it, these people were mad as fuck that they couldn't catch me by using legal channels so they've resorted to immoral tactics like entrapment. I find their dealings sometimes no better than the criminals I fought so hard to bring down. That's why I refuse to work with certain organizations, why I shunned them, because of their unethical practices.

Like this young woman they'd sent into my lair, the lion's den if you will with only her body and her wiles; they can spout all that bullshit about her mind but the bottom line is they're using her body, the whole package to lure me in like I'm some green boy. As if I'm some incompetent fuck to be led by my dick. I wouldn't be surprised if they expected her to fuck me if it came to that to achieve their goals, the question is was she willing to sacrifice herself for them?

She wants to play the game let her deal with the embarrassing questions; she already thinks I'm the lowest form of life there is, preying on innocent children so why should my less than stellar approach be such a surprise?

Now I've placed her in a dilemma; if she got up and stormed off that would end our acquaintance and she wouldn't gain anything; game, set, match; but if she stayed she ran the risk of giving me the impression that she was interested. I do have to give her points for keeping a cool head though, there were a few moments there when I was sure she wanted to throw her drink in my face.

Denise came back with the appetizer platter and a new glass for Cierra, it hadn't escaped my notice that she seemed a little out of sorts I'll have to have a word with her about her attitude around the customers. Cierra didn't seem too impressed by her either as I noticed a slight change in her body language.

"So what's it going to be?" I questioned as soon as we were alone again.

She took a deep swallow before lifting her eyes to mine; my gut clenched, there was definitely something going on behind those eyes of hers but even more than that was the pull I'd felt from the first moment I laid eyes on her photograph. She had something in her that pulled at the heart of me and regardless of the reasons for her being here I'm not going to stop until I'd explored all the possibilities. Let's hope we both made it out unscathed.

"I'm not sure how to answer your question I don't think I've ever been put in such a position before."

"What you're not accustomed to dealing with straightforward people? I find that hard to believe in this day and age with the way the world is moving."

"Straightforward is one thing Mr. Mancini I'm not sure that that's the word I'd use to describe what you are."

"Fair enough, you can of course choose to get up and walk away but then we'd never know what might've been would we?" She made me smile, all that banked fire just screaming to be released. Once the facade has been dropped and the pretense out of the way I'm going to revel in that fire in fact I'm looking forward to being singed by it.

Cierra

This isn't going at all the way I'd expected it to, I'm not some impressionable schoolgirl to be taken in by a pretty face or to be swayed by a suave tongue; but I must admit that he has something. There's a quality about him that pulls at you, draws you in, that to the point no bullshit what you see is what you get attitude.

Maybe that's how he's been able to elude the authorities all this time maybe his charm and charismatic personality leads others to look the other way; turn a blind eye to his true nature because as to date we have yet to find anyone who's willing to point a finger at this man; well except for a few of his bevy of ex-flings but their testimonies were so transparent even a first string law intern could destroy it in a court of law.

My inclination is to get up and walk away but what would I achieve? I'd have to engineer another chance meeting in the near future and that just smacked of desperation. The one thing Hank Mancini isn't is stupid, I have no doubt he'd see through anything I came up with; so I was left with only one choice; capitulation. I gritted my teeth as I thought of the best way to give in without seeming to be, if I stayed there's no doubt that he'd think I was interested in what he was offering; which has no place here Cierra you're doing your job remember? It doesn't matter what he thinks; but it did.

I cleared my throat and faced him head on, I'm sure the heat in my face was rather obvious but there was nothing for it unless I decided to hide behind my hair until I settled down again. I chose an olive from the tray the disgruntled server had brought with our drinks and popped it into my mouth to stall for time, didn't want to seem too eager after practically calling him a pig. I'll have to watch that in the future if he insisted on being this way, so...disarming.

Mancini

I'm just a little disappointed that she's giving in so easily she hasn't said anything as yet but her body language and that look in her eyes are enough of a giveaway. I'm sure her superiors have instructed her to take any and all necessary steps to get close to me but how far am I willing to let this go? How far is she?

The fact that I wanted her changed things; this is the first time in a long time that they've tried to get someone this close to me; sometimes it'll be a plant in one of my places but most of the time they had me under a microscope; that's when they had me under twenty four hour surveillance. This was a new tactic though and I hope she finds it just a little unsettling that they were all but prostituting her to serve their own purposes.

"Well, you still haven't answered my question Cierra, what's it going to be?"

"Is this how you usually pick up women, what if I'm not interested?"

"Are you?" I watched her squirm in her seat as she kept eye contact; the longer this went on the less guilt I felt for treating her this way. It didn't enter my mind that I was being just a tad bit irrational, after all she didn't know me outside of what she'd read in some files and even then what she knows is half-truths; but somehow it irritated the fuck out of me that she was here for this purpose; that she was making me fall for her when to her I was just a job. Of course she didn't know that I knew who she was; that led me to ponder how different things might've been if we'd met under less deceitful circumstances; Just a man and a beautiful woman.

"Why don't we just play it by ear Mr. Mancini?"

"Hank, I'd like you to call me Hank."

"Fine, Hank why don't we take it slow? I'm not interested in rushing into anything and anyway a man like you should be more careful about picking up strange women."

"A man like me?"

"You know, wealthy, single, you are single aren't you?"

"I wouldn't be propositioning you if I weren't."

"I'll take your word for it, so what do you say we take things at my pace?"

I watched her pretty much the way I imagined a predator watches the prey that he's trapped; we were playing two separate games here or at least I was. One was to best the secret agent at every turn, and the other was to lure the woman into my bed. I've never been one for easy task.

"That's not gonna work; I'll agree to taking things a little slow for now but it'll be at our pace that's only fair after all it involves both of us."

"Yes but you're the one who wants something from me."

"And if you didn't want something from me you'd be long gone." Touch that Ms. Stone.

"Though I find you rather brash I must admit to being slightly intrigued so I guess I'll keep you company a little while longer."

I bet that took a lot for you to admit.

Chapter 9

Cierra

He didn't seem too surprised by my answer. Cocky bastard! He just smiled at me and took another sip of his drink. I snagged another olive from the platter more for something to do with my hands than anything else while he watched me over the lip of his snifter.

No wonder he had such a reputation with women if he treated them all to his brand of potency. Even knowing what I knew of him or what was suspected in any case, I still find myself inexplicably drawn to his magnetism. He was without a doubt the most gorgeous human being I'd ever met and there was no doubt that had I been that girl in another time I might have indulged my stupid girl heart but there was no way. I had a job to do and if I did it well the man sitting across from me will be sitting in a jail cell for a long long time.

"That's big of you Cierra, so tell me something nonthreatening about yourself since my questions seem to bother you so much."

"There's not much to tell. I'm new here from a small town in Georgia."

"Where in Georgia?"

"Why? I'm sure you've never heard of it." And for a man of your resources I'm sure it wouldn't take you long to unravel the truth if you went looking.

"You'd be surprised at what I know, try me."

Shit, we'd come up with a fictitious place of course but somehow I didn't trust this, somehow I just knew he'd go looking.

"It's a little place called Blythe."

"You're right, never heard of it."

We talked for the next few hours about inconsequential things and I began to relax a little. Once he stopped with the panty dropping innuendos, Hank Mancini was a very intelligent and quite enigmatic man; a very dangerous combination given the circumstances.

Mancini

We ended the night with the understanding that we'd take the time to get to know each other and see if there was anything there to explore. It was a bone for her no doubt, I'm sure she was thinking she'd survived her first face-to-face with the monster and though she hadn't learned anything incriminating she'd found an in; one I'd given her because obviously I'd lost my fucking mind. Sniffing around a damn federal agent. Way to go Mancini she'll probably end up fucking you in more ways than one.

I watched her walk away after rejecting my offer to at least see her to her car; special agent Stone has a first class ass.

Cierra

I spent the next day going over everything I knew about Hank Mancini when I wasn't replaying the events of the night before over and over again in my head. I still couldn't shake the feeling that we were missing something; I couldn't reconcile the straightforward plain speaking sex symbol of the night before with the child trafficking criminal we'd been after for a decade.

Maybe it's because the others who came after him before were men, that's why they missed it or it could be that as a woman I looked at things a little differently; hopefully it had nothing to do with my disgusting and unprofessional attraction to him. It's as well that I wouldn't be giving my report face-to-face or the blush that I was sure covered my face at just the thought of him would be a dead giveaway.

I was due to call Director Durant for a briefing in a few minutes and the truth is I have nothing; at least nothing new to add except my suspicions that we were on the wrong track somehow and it was too soon to go there. I couldn't very well tell my superior that I found myself drawn to a suspect for the first time in my short career and I somehow couldn't see him doing the things we thought him guilty of.

I stared at the picture I'd taken with my butterfly pin last night; my heart did that funny little thing it seems to do only for him which is becoming a little worrisome for me. I can't do my job effectively if I'm sidetracked by this unwanted attraction. Wouldn't it be just great if I lost all credibility my first time out in the field because I couldn't see pass his handsome face and winning ways?

"Who are you really Hank Mancini and why can't I get you out of my head?"

Chapter 10

Mancini

"The fuck?" I awoke from a deep sleep where I'd been caught in a dream of twists and turns; she was in turn chasing me and running away, enticing me with her beauty. Each time I drew near she evaded my touch laughing all the while until I finally brought her down in the garden of all places. That's when I woke up just when things were about to get interesting.

A cold shower was in order but that'll have to come after I had done some more research on the woman who'd invaded my dreams. If she was going to follow me even into the dream world I'd better get a better handle on her.

JORDAN SILVER | 167

I did a more in-depth search on
Ms. Cierra Stone going back deeper
into her childhood I'd only glossed
over it before in my first investigation
but now it was almost as though I
needed to know all. Now I looked not
with the eyes of a target but with the
eyes of a man who was interested in a
woman.

She hadn't had it very easy at all
as a kid and the more I read the clearer
she became; losing her family at such a
young age and in such a horrific way
must've scarred her somewhat I'm
sure. The report on her family's
murders didn't say too much about the
young girl who'd been left behind. The
fact that the perpetrator had never been
caught and her subsequent enrollment
into the bureau all these years later
spoke volumes.

"You have a bone to pick don't
you little girl?"

It was very clichéd but still I
understood the drive, the need for

vengeance. Maybe after our business has been squared away I'll help her on her hunt. I felt a pang for the little girl who had lost so much so young; what would she say if she knew that my life was about helping others who were just as she'd been? Helpless and alone.

I spent a long time studying her, trying to gauge just what it was about her that drew me. Was it the eyes? No I don't think so, I've seen beautiful eyes before; was it the tilt of her mouth, those wide sensuous lips that just begged to be licked? Whatever it was I was looking forward to exploring, no matter how our business with each other unfolded, one thing was certain; the delectable Ms. Stone was going to be under me one way or the other.

The buzzing of my door intercom on a Saturday morning could only mean one thing family; I watched on the security monitor as my two brothers entered my private elevator. I didn't have to think too hard to find their reasons for being here at this early hour. Adrien was the oldest of the three of us by a scant month and a half, I came next then Jaxxon. We'd met in grade school when some fucker had been bullying Jaxxon who was a puny little thing back then. I'd jumped into the fray after having spent the past week watching the same thing unfold time and time again.

The bully whose name escapes me now would corner Jaxx and torment him until he gave up his lunch money. Then the poor little thing would sit there while everyone else ate just looking lost. Well that day I'd had about all I could stand and I'd jumped in; pretty soon Adrien had cone out of nowhere and had joined in the fracas and between the three of us we'd put a beating on his overgrown ass. From that day to this we've been together through thick and thin; it hadn't been long after that day that my parents had adopted the two boys into the family since their home lives left much to be desired.

Adrien's mother was a drunk who'd only remembered she had a son when she needed him to make a run to the liquor store; sometimes at all hours of the night. My father had put a stop to that shit when he threatened to have the place shut down for serving a minor. Jaxxon's dad thought it was fun to use him as a punching bag and sometimes ashtray; it only took Juliet Mancini one time seeing the telltale signs of the young boy's abuse before he was packed up and moved in. Adrien followed not long after when one of his mother's Johns thought he could take out what she couldn't deliver on Adrien. He'd escaped out of

JORDAN SILVER | 171

a window and hotfooted it to our house and there he'd stayed.

"What's up guys your wives kick you out or what?"

"Funny bro...so?" Adrien dropped down on the couch while Jaxx went towards the minibar to get some sparkling water. He threw each of us one before settling next to Adrien on the couch.

"So what?" Of course I knew what they were after but I enjoyed busting their chops every chance I got.

"Don't fuck around bro we know you met with the undercover Fed last night how did it go?"

It was always Jaxx's way to let Adrien take the lead, me I'm always the one stirring shit up and making them both crazy.

"What, you didn't hack into the system to get a look at the report?"

"She hasn't sent anything in yet I'm dying to see if she's as good as they say."

"Jaxx you're rather quiet what's on your mind buddy?"

"I hope you know what you're doing bro getting close to this chick; why didn't you just tell her you knew who she was and be done with

it?"

"How do you know I didn't?"

"Our wives got the low down that's why we are here at the ass crack of dawn; Wilson know what the fuck you're up to?"

"I don't answer to Wilson you know that."

"I know you're a hard headed son of a bitch who's more trouble than he's worth; what game are you playing now?"

"Adrien you worry too much you're worse than a mother hen, Cierra's no threat to me."

I saw Jaxx studying me out the side of my eye and I already knew what he was looking for; If I gave them the slightest hint that I was even remotely interested in this woman they'd be on me in a heartbeat. My brothers were very overprotective of me they were the only ones outside of the organization who knew what it was that I really did, not even my parents have that privilege because I'm afraid it might put mama in an early grave. They knew my life wouldn't be worth shit if word ever got out and they also knew I had no intentions of ever letting that happen.

"I don't know Hank this is very dangerous always before they operated from afar, this time they're right on your doorstep and you're letting them in. If Adrien hadn't gotten a whiff of what was going down you'd be walking blind and from what I hear the sparks were definitely flying between you two last night."

"Scorching hot's what I heard."

"Your wives are nosy as fuck."

"Stop evading brother what the fuck are you doing bro?" Adrien and his impatient ass was like a dog with a bone.

I'm not in the habit of keeping shit from my brothers it's the bro code or at least it's ours but if I let them in now it could open a whole slew of shit that I wasn't quite ready to deal with, still I didn't want to start keeping shit from my boys especially not while pulling the tiger's tail.

"I like her."

You could hear a pin drop as the two of them looked back and forth between each other before turning back to me.

"You like her!"

"Yeah Adrien I like her."

"Like really like her?"

"Yeah Jaxx, really likc hcr."

"Fuck!"

"Yeah Adrien that about sums it up."

"Are we talking Juliet Mancini's dinner table on a Sunday like? Or your usual two months is the cutoff like?"

That was the question wasn't it? One I've been asking myself which in itself was grounds for fear; I'm a solitary animal by nature, but in my dealings with the fairer sex I've always been more aloof, more careful if you will. I didn't intend to be trapped in anyone's web and besides my lifestyle did not lend to the whole settling down thing. For some reason when I look into her eyes that all changes.

"I'm not sure bro."

They did that exchanging of looks thing again before both hanging their heads; it came to mind that they did that a lot when dealing with me, even while we were kids.

"You can never do anything the easy way can you bro? Fuck this is gonna be a shit storm; I better keep my nose to the grindstone so I can keep your ass out of a sling because chances are if you're gone over this woman you'll be ass stupid in no time and making fucked up mistakes that might get your ass either killed or in jail."

"Never happen bro." I had to laugh at his assessment, what he described just wasn't me at all.

"Tell him Jaxxon since he thinks he knows it all."

"It's true bro, the right woman gets her hooks into you you lose all sense of anything for a while until you have them locked down and you can breathe again, then things start to right themselves. Since you're at the starting gate it's going to be a while yet before you exit the danger zone."

"I never said she was the right woman for me." And why did the sound of that make me feel...whole? That's it, the idea that she could be it which should make me run for cover actually made me feel good. Fuck.

"The fact that you said you didn't know was answer enough bro, we know you; if she was like the others we wouldn't even be having this conversation. I can't wait to meet her now, the one woman who's going to bring the great Mancini to his knees. You better not wait too long to introduce her to mama, that's a whole other shit storm you do not want to walk through."

"I think you've lost your mind." I felt, not fear but something, something new and unfamiliar that unfurled in the pit of my stomach. They couldn't be right, I was attracted to Cierra yes, okay very attracted but there's no way I was ready to go there. Was I?

"Sure bro keep telling yourself that."

"We just met, there's no way I'm going there." Was that my voice sounding almost desperate, the fuck?

"Sabra and I were married three months after we met, Adrien and Star lasted about four, what makes you think you're gonna be any different?"

"Uh because I'm not pussy whipped like you two freaks, no woman is going to change my well ordered life, I've already got shit mapped out and a wife and kids just aren't part of the equation, not while I still have work to do."

"Even superman had a love interest." Jaxxon smirked at me I know they were enjoying this, though what this was I still wasn't quite sure. When these two had met and fallen in love with their respective wives I'd given them hell yes, but this was different, this wasn't the happily ever after that they'd found with their women, this was just a simple case of lust. There that felt better as long as I remembered what was really going on here I was fine. Yes the lust for her was stronger than in the past but that didn't mean anything. Nothing had changed, I'm still the same Hank Mancini that I'd been before I'd ever heard the name Cierra Stone.

"We'll see, thanks for looking out bros but I'm good, I'll leave the pansy ass shit to you two, speaking of which Adrien that wife of yours a pain in the ass."

"Uh huh, and what would you like me to do about it?"

"Get her off my ass for one, that'll be a good start."

"No thanks, if she's giving you shit that means it's my week off you're on your own brother."

"Gee thanks you're all heart if you two can't control your women what makes you think I want that fucking headache?"

"Because what we do control makes it all worthwhile, you'll see lil brother it wont be long now." They both thought that shit was funny as they headed for the door. I was already deep in thought before they'd cleared the foyer; they couldn't be right could they? No way.

I had to put personal matters aside for the rest of the day; this latest operation was a little tricky. The cargo was bigger than my usual haul so the transference was going to take longer not to mention the usual language barrier. I'm fluent in many languages including Mandarin so no problem but some of my crew weren't as proficient in the language; add the obvious fear that these poor young girls will be under after weeks in deplorable conditions and things could get FUBAR quickly. It's my job to prevent that from happening, to see that everything went off without a hitch and most importantly that there was no lost of innocent lives.

I had no more time left to finalize things this was it, and with this sort of operation every second counts. I couldn't afford to be distracted now I'll have time enough to think about the beautiful Cierra later. We were meeting for drinks tomorrow night after all.

Chapter 11

Cierra

I got myself together put all my ducks in a row so to speak before contacting the handler for now I'm reporting directly to Durant since this case was top priority. The bureau had already spent numerous man-hours not to mention the funds it cost to keep men on Mancini around the clock for so many years.

There were rumblings about pulling back since we kept failing in all our endeavors to trap him but someone somewhere had a hard on for this guy because we still kept going. I was beginning to think this was a fool's errand, too early to tell for sure but either my instincts were way off which I doubted or we have been after the wrong man for over a decade.

There's no mistake that he's up to something and what that something is I'll hopefully find out, but there's no way the Hank Mancini I met the night before was a child trafficker, I'd bet my shiny new badge on it. I took a deep breath and prepared to give my report as it were. The director answered on the first ring as if he'd been waiting on the call.

"Agent Stone you got something for me?"

"Not exactly sir; the preliminary meeting went well but he didn't go for the bait so we're on to Plan B."

"Well we always knew that might be the way things headed from the get go so no surprises there; so you've met the man, your take?"

I was afraid he was going to ask me that; I didn't really have an answer not one I could share with him anyway but his voice sounded so excited, so sure that I was going to be the one to finally get the results they were hoping for.

"I think I'm going to need a little more time before I can form any type of opinion sir. Mr. Mancini is no fool I didn't think he would be too forthcoming on the first acquaintance but he did express..." I cut myself off I knew what he would say but I couldn't help feeling resentment. Had I been a man this would never have come up but because I'm a female and a passable one at that it was quite alright to expect me to use my body and female charm to lure the suspected criminal into my web.

"He did express what agent Stone?"

I took a fortifying breath before continuing on. "He expressed an interest in me personally."

"That's good, that's very good; we did tell you that that was the best course of action. I think we've always failed before because we were never able to get too close to the guy it's like he has a sixth sense or something but a skirt; now that's a different kettle of fish."

Pig! I resented all of them including Mancini for putting me in this position and I still wasn't sure that he hadn't been playing some type of cat and mouse game with me the night before. I'd gotten the distinct feeling last night that he'd been playing me but why? None of the Intel showed him to be that way with the females he usually took to his bed. He's reportedly very generous and somewhat attentive for a playboy. I knew his adopted brothers were agents very well noted ones at that but anything to do with Mancini was purposely kept out of their knowing, so there was no way he could know who I was and yet I couldn't shake the feeling that he was one step ahead of me somehow.

"So when are you seeing him again?"

Durant's over excited tone brought me out of my reverie.

"Tomorrow night we're having drinks in the evening; how about his detail anything there?"

"Yeah there's some movement but it's the usual nothing we can really use, we think he might have secret exits in and out of his places because we never really see him with anyone but we know he's meeting with these people and since the asshole judge has prohibited us from trespassing on Mancini's properties in an official capacity we can't really get eyes and ears in them so you're it kid. If you could keep your eyes and ears open when you gain his trust that might be just what we need because so far this guy is kicking our asses and the higher ups are making noises about scrapping the entire operation, which would be a real shame considering all the time and money we've already spent."

"Yeah I was wondering about that." I wasn't so sure that Mancini was as gullible as Durant seemed to think where I was concerned, wherever they'd gotten the notion that a man who had evaded law enforcement for so long would be putty in my hands for the mere fact that I was a woman was ludicrous. I didn't see him just revealing his secrets; whatever this guy had going on he was very efficient at keeping it under wraps, it was going to take a lot of hard work on my part to break through that and I wasn't so sure after finally meeting him that that was going to be as easy as I'd first thought.

I remembered Gracie's warning to not be too cocky going in, how that attitude had caused many others before me to fail. Looks like this one was going to take longer than expected. It was going to take all my considerable skills to bring down the great Mancini, if that were even possible.

The question is did I want to? Yes I had a job to do but was I really doing that job if I let others dictate what I should believe? Something inside of me was very against the idea of his being guilty of the things we'd put on him; if he wasn't guilty of the list of criminal activities we suspected him of then what? Because when all was said and done Hank Mancini has been up to something for the past decade or more; problem is no one seems to know exactly what that was.

I spent the next few minutes on the phone going over strategy with my boss while feeling slightly sick to my stomach. I had a weird feeling that I was about to embark on a very twisted journey full of pitfalls and stumbling blocks. Things were not as cut and dry as they appeared to be and as much as Hank Mancini grated on me the wrong way there was no denying he made me feel. Boy did he make me feel.

I spent yet another day going over everything I knew about him while wishing I could just join the crew on surveillance detail. I know what his life looks like on paper I was very well acquainted with his every supposed crime home and abroad but there was no real insight into the real man.

His files were surprisingly lacking in that area for someone who'd been under the scope of most of the law-enforcement agencies of the world for so many years. This only helped to add to the suspicion; more was known about the Presidents' daily doings than this guy who was under constant surveillance twenty four seven and from many different factions at that. It's almost like he really was smoke able to enter into any place undetected and exit the same.

We'd searched for disguises the one time we were able to get close enough to plant devices in his place but there had been no evidence to suggest he went that route. Durant's speculation that there might be secret doors had some merit but it would be a while before this guy let me anywhere remotely close to finding that out if ever. Somehow I didn't see him opening up that side of his life to a complete stranger no matter how much he professed to want to take me to his bed.

Mancini

I have to be smart here I couldn't afford any screw –ups, there was no real danger of her learning anything useful to take back to her people but still there's always room for error. Always before I've been very careful to keep my private life separate from my business, with her I'm straddling both sides of the fence. To her I am business, for now; I'll exact retribution for that as well when the time comes. The fact that I wanted her and indeed planned to have her barring death did not in anyway erase the truth of our beginning. She'd come to me to deceive I'm not the type to let that slide.

She'd no doubt made her report by now I wonder what she'd had to tell Durant about our first meeting? No doubt the other man thought it was a great coup for them that she'd got to me. They've never been this close before and my brothers were right, if they hadn't given me the heads up and she'd come into my place as she had I would've been naturally drawn to her, but what might've become of that is anybody's guess.

I'm not an inexperienced youth on his first walk around the block I wouldn't have been giving up any secrets even then, but it still could've made for a dangerous situation. No one but my brothers knew the ins and outs of my operation not even Jace knew all of it and neither did Wilson, there were things that I kept close to my chest being the untrusting soul that I am. The women I'd dealt with in the past never breached my outer shell enough to reach that part of me that would cause me to open up that side of my life so there'd never been any danger of that happening before.

With Cierra, knowing who she was and what she was after, feeling the things that I'm feeling for her; it could pose a bit of a problem but nothing I can't handle. I just wish she hadn't come into my life at this particular time when I have this very delicate case on my hands. Instead of devoting all of my time to her acquisition I now have to divide it between her and making sure my ass is covered with these guys. I was cutting it kind of close too pulling off the raid tonight and meeting with her tomorrow night knowing that her people were even now watching my every move or trying to but that's the way I usually do things I like to live on the edge.

Once again I got my mind ready, releasing all the unnecessary data from my memory bank so I could focus all my energies on the task at hand. There were ten no doubt very scared young women depending on me to rescue them from a fate almost certainly

worst than death though they did not
know I existed.

I had to set things up with my guys before going in because once I boarded the ship I had to be in constant motion and we couldn't afford to miss a step once we got the ball rolling. There was most definitely going to be firepower exchanged; my job was to see that none of the innocents were caught in the crossfire. I hated losing any of the unfortunates on my watch and so far I've been lucky where others haven't.

This cargo was made up of young girls who were bound to be terrified; one of my operatives is a female who specializes in these matters, we've done enough of these runs that we're almost expert by now but there was always an unknown element that could pop up out of nowhere. In the old days we would've just rushed the shit and taken the hostages by force, there would most likely be lives lost, among them some of the victims.

These days we handled things with just a bit more sophistication; I have accrued a reputation as a dealer so to speak, I'm known all over the world in some less than exemplary circles as the man to go to if you want to get things done. I deal in weapons, drugs, humans you name it I do it. The reason my operations are so smooth is because I pay very close attention to detail, I set things up so that no one outside of the parties involved ever know that I've been there. I do not leave a calling card no imprint of my existence or involvement is ever left behind.

By the time my so-called new friends feel the pinch they have no idea who it was that put the squeeze on them. It's kept me alive all this time and the fact that law enforcement was always on my ass added credibility to my cred as a dangerous criminal who was able to outsmart them at every turn. My criminal element was very impressed with my track record, if only the feds knew how their constant hounding kept me in business. Criminals liked nothing better than seeing one of their own getting over on the 'man'.

Doing what I do is not easy, it takes time and patience and a strong sense of justice and though I might not wear a suit of armor or have supernatural skills, I have honed what I do have to almost perfection because I can't afford to fail, ever. I never expected that my life would turn out this way; I'd always thought I'd follow in my father's footsteps and go into business, but when I was old enough to know better I realized I had no real interest in business, it was too structured if you will.

No I needed more of a challenge that didn't always come down to dollars and cents. I was extremely wealthy at the end of my eighteenth birthday, while my peers were being given the hottest new car I was being handed the key to the safety deposit box that held all the pertinent information about my inheritance from my paternal grandfather, a man whom I had loved and who had showered me always with kindness which extended even from the grave.

My parents weren't too worried that I would run wild and do all the things that usually got guys like me in trouble, they'd taught me well. No instead I set up a trust for my two brothers who had bitched and moaned about it but it had fallen on deaf ears. We were in it together my brothers and I and there was no way I could see myself having and they not. We went to different schools because believe it or not they'd always wanted law enforcement, maybe because of their shitty upbringings they thought this was a good way to help kids who were in the same predicament as they'd been in before my parents took over, they knew the signs they claimed which made them perfect for their professions.

I on the other hand still under the assumption that I was going to take over the running of my family's vast corporation had headed off to business school. Who knew then how far removed from that world I would become in such a short space of time? Or how effortlessly I would slide into it. My way was nowhere near what my brothers were doing, they went the route of the textbook while I came at it from the dark side so to speak. I had no idea when I embarked on my little venture that things would turn out the way they have, that my life would be forever changed and that the once care free youth with not a worry in the world would become the man I am today. I single handedly built my own world of crime from nothing, drawing in some of the world's most elusive criminals and I did it all from behind a computer screen.

It's quite simple really I
concocted a scheme and carried it out
in minute detail, a scheme in which I
was both buyer and seller of arms an
arms dealer if you will. It's almost like
a Ponzi scheme but here's how I
worked it. First I kept my ears peeled
for anything to do with my newfound
interest and when I'd gotten a whiff of
something interesting I went to work. I
set myself up as someone who wanted
to buy arms and made sure that
information got to the right circles.

Then I faked a different ID to set
up myself as a seller of arms and that
was it, nothing had exchanged hands
obviously but after a few of those
transactions the right people had taken
notice and pretty soon I was being
approached by both buyers and sellers.
This opened communications between
me and the underground criminal
community which eventually got me
an entrée into the world of high crime

and from there it spread from one criminal faction to the next.

I did this at the ripe old age of nineteen one day when I'd been bored out of my fucking mind studying economics at Wharton. I knew by then that I had no real interest in going into the family business that my dad and his dad before him were so proud of but neither did I know what the hell I wanted to do with my life.

At first I was amazed at how easy it had been to get my foot in the door, I just basically set myself up as a player, invented a whole new identity for myself and that was it. It's amazingly easy to reinvent yourself as long as you have the money and the resources and no place has more resources than the quads of an Ivy league school where the nation's best and brightest were being cultivated to run the world; after all it's not the little deadbeat drug dealer on the corner selling to school kids that's running the show, it's the one providing him with the goods. That's where I focused my scheme, not on the middleman but straight to the top. It was better to cut off the head than the tail.

I had no real direction in mind when I first started out, it was just a test for myself to see if I could do it, there were always stories of how easily people had gained access to certain things in our society, things that they should never have had access to or even in some cases have known about, but every other day there was another story of espionage or some kid in his mother's basement cracking codes or damn near bringing down nations. I took my time and nurtured relationships with the men and women I'd drawn into my web still not knowing where I was going with all this but just simply blown away by how easy it all was, not to mention how high up corruption went in our little universe.

Pretty soon I was sitting around the table with dignitaries and men in high places brokering deals between nations, all hidden from the watchful eye of the public of course. It was then I learned my distrust of government agencies, I saw the way they did things, how they were willing to cut deals with unsavory characters in order to bring down what they considered to be the top dog. I believe in making them all pay.

When I'd first been approached by Wilson, I'd been very suspicious of him as well; it had taken him almost a year to wear me down and it was only after the realization that the thing I'd created had become bigger than I that I'd given in and called Wilson.

When I'd met Jace, Jace was more into the physical aspect back then than I, I was the brain to his brawn. I'd learned more then about the secret society that worked behind the scenes, an organization that had been in existence for centuries, governed by men of certain families of which Wilson's was the leading faction. They spent their lives from generation to generation fighting injustice here and abroad.

Like me they trusted no government or the handpicked henchmen that made up their agencies. I guess you could say we were the police police. We play by a different set of rules that were all made with the welfare of the less fortunate in mind. Our motto is 'By any means necessary'.

Most of our enemies never saw the inside of a jail and that's why we're able to survive so long without anyone on the outside ever having the slightest inclination that we existed. We annihilate the guilty and on the rare occasion that we let them live because of their ignorance of the facts or something of the like, they never knew what the hell had hit them in the first place.

So you see, it's hard for me coming from that place to find myself drawn to someone who one of those agencies were now hailing as their brightest and best. The one saving grace is that I'm her first real job; maybe they haven't had time to corrupt her as yet or at least that's what I'm hoping for because if she was going to be in my life for longer than two months as Adrien had so eloquently pointed out she was going to have to be a hell of a lot better than anything their corrupt asses could produce.

I'd already done recon on the harbor where the ship was docking in a couple hours barring emergency. The freighter they had chosen was usually used to haul machine parts for industrial factories; some of these tankers usually have hidden compartments below deck that even the Coast Guard weren't aware of unless they'd had some prior warning.

Criminals had become more and more adept in this age of technology; it wasn't as easy as it once had been to catch them at their craft, so the craftier they got the more innovative guys like me had to become. It was a vicious cycle that never seemed to end, each time we made progress the criminal element came up with other ways to do what they did so it was a struggle always to keep on top of things.

My job tonight is to rescue the hostages and remove them to the secret location that has already been set up and waiting for them. The men and women who had paid to have them stolen and brought here will never lay eyes on them. It was a job best done under cover of darkness when the harbor was asleep and the necessary parties had been paid to look the other way.

On the off chance that such a payoff proved impossible or when difficult we usually just resorted to causing diversions elsewhere to keep the guards well away while we borrowed time to do what we had to. For tonight's little episode we'd bought some time from one of our contacts on the inside. The coast would be clear long enough for us to do what needed to be done and be gone in the wind.

I'd garnered such a reputation as a criminal that the people who came looking for my services trusted me to choose whichever venue I thought best to get their particular job done. If all went well hopefully by tomorrow all the men involved will either be dead or finding themselves afoul of the law for something that had nothing to do with tonight's operation. The children my crew and I were about to rescue will be returned to their homes in due time if they were proven to be favorable conditions, if that wasn't the case then other arrangements would be made for them. It's the way we always did things when kids were involved one of my stipulations to be exact.

Everything was in place and ready to go, every detail had been finalized; we'd tried as usual to prepare for every contingency but I never rested easy until an Op was completely over. Whenever I headed an Op I tried my best to bring everyone out alive, my record has been stellar so far and that's why I'm the one most tapped for this kind of job within the organization.

As the clock wound down I put aside everything else but the job; I'd chosen my team from beginning to end; most of the crew on the cargo ship was part of my team but some were unknowns. Criminals aren't the most trusting bunch of assholes after all and although they'd commissioned me to handle the whole job except for the kidnapping of the girls, they still wanted to have some of their own men on hand overseeing everything.

My men and women who took the voyage over with them would've spent their time wisely if they were doing their jobs gathering info, wiretapping their communications, and safeguarding against any unwelcome circumstances that might arise. The most dangerous part of the operation will take place in the next hour or so, that's when we attempt to rescue the hostages and detain the traffickers without loss of life to the victims while keeping the criminals from contacting anyone with an alert, you never know what other outside forces might be involved when dealing with men of this caliber and it was always best to cover all the bases and be prepared for every contingency.

Now here's the tricky part, since the men who'd hired me and in fact had orchestrated the kidnappings at the behest of the sick fuck wealthy men and women were known dignitaries it's not so simple to just dust them and be done with it. Some embassy is bound to notice that their ambassador is missing. We could always bring them up on charges but the old diplomatic immunity thing might allow them to slip through loop holes somehow, and there was no point in giving them over to their own government for justice because this shit reached to the top and there was never really anyone who could be trusted.

For this particular operation because of the delicate matter involved, young girls who had been stolen from their families; we'd come up with something a little more elaborate for all its simplicity. Getting rid of the filth on the ship was no big deal they were just low rung lackeys. As for the men who'd hired me I'd insisted they take ownership of the merchandise at a prearranged location; too bad they were never going to make it there.

I received the signal from my men aboard the ship that they were approaching the harbor. Jace was already in place on a boat a few slips away from where the ship was supposed to dock. The Coast Guard as earlier prearranged was out of sight and the harbor clear of even light traffic. I stood on the pier a lone figure dressed all in black a very B movie cliché to be sure. As they pulled in and went about the business of dropping anchor I communicated with the Captain who would soon become the first casualty of the night. I saw the spray of blood across his chest before his body dropped. Good job Jace.

There was suddenly a lot of movement on deck, which is what we wanted I went into motion while chaos ensued on board. I knew where the cargo hold was and that's where I was headed, my only interest in getting those girls out of there. The rest of my team was in charge of keeping the enemy occupied. They had no idea where the attack came from, as there had been no official call to surrender, and no known threat onboard. I had no doubt my team was doing what we did best as I made my way efficiently towards my goal.

I felt no sense of loss for the men who were even now no doubt losing their lives our purpose was not to populate the world's prisons with the parasites that preyed on the weak so they could deplete the resources and sap the energies of law-abiding citizens. No our aim is to eliminate them once and for all; no deals, no backhanded slaps on the wrists. It was not an easy thing to make those decisions, in the beginning I struggled, it amounted to me ending lives after all; but after seeing what I've seen for so long I could do no other. These beasts would not stop otherwise it was a sad fact of nature that some men were vicious conscienceless predators who excelled in preying on the weak and the defenseless.

"Jace I'm in." I spoke into the High-tech sports watch that came equipped with everything from camera to a mike.

"You're covered bro Drake and Shawna have you flanked, and the others are moving in on their targets as we speak."

I made my way to the hold; intelligence had alerted me to the fact that there was always a man down there with the captives. I have to first neutralize him and then get the ten young no doubt scared girls up and out. Since there was only one way out there was no way for me to take him by surprise so I had to move in and strike in one swift motion.

Daniel one of our special tech gurus had found a way to plant eyes inside without being detected so I was able to watch the guard on my watch screen with just the turn of the stem.

Good, he seemed a little nervous by the rushing feet above and since their communications had been jammed by now there was no answer to his repeated calls. Looks like he was about to make my job easier by leaving the hold; he made his way towards the ladder obviously headed topside to see what all the commotion was about. At least I didn't have to knife him in front of the innocent eyes of the children being held there.

I waited for my target behind and slightly off to the side of the trap door he would soon emerge from so I could attack before being sighted. He'd barely cleared the door before I was jerking him up and back forcefully, snapping his neck between my hands effortlessly. I eased his body down behind some crates in the off chance that one of his cohorts escaped the melee and came to assist. Their orders were to annihilate the captives if there was a rescue attempt, something I was not about to let happen.

"The hold is clear Jace am I clear to go?"

"Pick up is in place it's a go; the team has neutralized the others, they're on their way to you now."

That was easy but then again that's the way it usually is when you have a very well coordinated team of dedicated people working together.

I eased the trapdoor up and made my way down.

"I come in peace." I said the words in their native tongue so they wont be afraid; it had only been a few weeks since their ordeals begun but already I could see the wear and tear on their young faces. Fear of the unknown would do that to anyone and in a child it was magnified.

I pulled out the official looking badge that I had hidden beneath my shirt; it's really just a seal with the organization's crest but to the naked eye it appears official. Their sighs of relief and exclamations proved positive that it worked. I didn't even bother shushing their excitement as I'd been assured that their captors had been dealt with effectively.

Starting with the littlest one I led them up the ladder and passed them off to Natasha, another one of my team who spoke mandarin. I'd sent in a few females on this run for obvious reasons, it hadn't been too hard to convince my hirers that with female presence the Op would go smoother and since I'm always given leave to form my own team when working for someone and this is something that's known in the dark world I play in, they didn't question me too closely.

"Jace we're headed topside any movement?" There was a pause before he answered giving the all clear.

"You're clear bro fifteen minutes to spare."

"We're moving."

The girls will be moved to a secure location where they will be checked over by a physician, fed and spoiled a little before we reached out to their families but first they needed to be debriefed to gain any and all pertinent information they may have about their abductions. If all was clear and their families hadn't played a part in their disappearances then we'd make provisions to return them.

We'd then start the process of investigating their respective families just because someone got on the television and cried over the disappearance of their child or loved one didn't necessarily mean that they were innocent of any wrongdoing in said disappearance. We took that shit seriously as none of us especially myself wanted to be responsible for returning a child to dangerous or deplorable conditions.

Yet another team member was tasked with captaining the now unmanned vessel to a before decided upon location where the bodies will be dropped off. The vessel itself will be stripped and renamed for its next voyage as it had been on all the others it had made in the past. I hopped into the back of the van with Tasha and the girls while Drake drove; I wasn't surprised to find them laughing at some little tidbit Tasha had shared with them.

I kept my silence as I sat and watched reading their body language looking for any signs of distress. I made it a point that my job didn't just end with the rescue I kept up with my victims and they all had ways of keeping in touch with me. Funnily enough they all chose to, these girls would be no different.

The other team I had in play to end things on this Op should be making contact by the time we reached the safe house. I wanted to make sure the girls were completely safe before we did anything else. There's no doubt that if these men lived they will do anything to keep their part in this crime secret which included murder; it was also a known fact within the organization that most of them had ties to if not in fact were members of organized crime. These factions are some of the most vicious in the world and would not think twice about snuffing out the lives of young innocents, they're the reason men like me exists, we're the complete opposite of them and their destructive forces in the world.

It was hours before we got the girls settled; I was pissed all over again to find that the youngest was barely ten fucking years old I mean what the fuck?

Team B had called in two hours ago with the news that the town car carrying the three delegates had met an unfortunate hiccup; the shit was already all over the news media. If all had gone as planned there will be no backdraft, it would appear as a freak accident started from a faulty engine. The fact that all three men were together shouldn't raise too many eyebrows as they were from the same nation but even if it did there was nothing leading back to the organization.

The final roundup will include the buyers who were expecting delivery of their merchandise within the next few days. The eight men and two women who were willing to shell out millions for the acquisition of human flesh were about to have their lives very disrupted. Where crimes not associated with the girls did not exist air- tight ones had been fabricated; they were all sown up nice and tight for a nice long stretch behind bars. That's if the justice system did its job.

I fell into bed feeling relieved; another job well done I'd already spoken to Wilson who as the sitting director of the Guardians like to be kept abreast of all recue missions. As head of the organization his job is to see to any loose ends, make the necessary contacts with the families and keep the government agencies in the dark. A tall order all around but he's been doing it for longer than I've been alive and he excels at it.

It wasn't long before she was once again plaguing me, now with the filth of the day behind me I could turn to more pleasant things. I replayed everything from the moment I first saw her standing in my place trying so hard but yet looking so out of place. I caught myself smiling there in the dark as I remembered her face when I'd shocked her with my boldness and the way she'd barely restrained herself from throwing her wine in my face. I didn't question it when I found myself jumping out of bed and getting dressed once more; I was about to do something I've never done before in my life but I believe strongly in going with my gut and that's what I'm doing now. Let's hope the agent doesn't pump my ass full of lead for my efforts.

Chapter 12

Mancini

She was staying in a townhouse in the heart of the city as part of her cover, which was as an up-and-coming socialite. Her background check looked pretty good: a young woman of means from a high-powered family. Of course it's one of those obscure families that no one ever heard of who just happens to be loaded. She's an alum of Vassar, at least that much is true, guess they had to keep some things as close to the truth as possible.

But as for the pseudo family, that was all fabrication. The ride downtown in my Ascari on the deserted streets took less than twenty minutes. I parked a few blocks away and took the back street sticking to the shadows. I had no problem leaving my million and a half dollar car on the streets of lower Manhattan because the shit was secured tighter than Fort Knox.

Her place was on the end with a balcony and a privacy fence, which made gaining entrance easy for someone with my particular skills. I left my shoes on the balcony as I picked the lock that led into the living area, my nifty little device made easy work of her alarm system and I was in being as careful as possible as I made my way through her temporary residence making sure to stick to the shadows once more.

I scanned for any hidden cameras or other detectors with this nifty little gadget Jace had built that was perfect for not only detecting but jamming those things as well. I didn't know if her people had her under surveillance or not but I wasn't taking any chances. It was one thing for me to accept that she was fast becoming my weakness and quite another for others to know.

I couldn't forget after all that I was dealing with a trained federal agent here. One other thing I hadn't taken into account was whether or not she would be alone, that thought brought me up short for a second. Nothing that I had uncovered hinted at a love interest but that didn't mean it wasn't a possibility. I folded my fists at the surge of emotion that overcame me at the thought I'll have to deal with that later. Right now I have to see her, be sure she was here alone, what the fuck I planned to do if she wasn't I had no idea I just knew I would punish her in some way if that's what I found. Fucked up I know but there you have it, I never claimed to be the most rational motherfucker out there.

The moonlight coming in through the bedroom window cast a shadowy glow over her perfect skin, her face serene in slumber looked even younger; my fingers itched to touch, to stroke her hair where it laid spread out over her pillow. Thank heavens she didn't sleep in the nude or else my control might've failed me; it was a trial as it was keeping my distance as her chest rose and fell with her easy breathing the T-shirt she wore to sleep in stretched taut across her breasts.

I don't know how long I stood there but I felt the tension of the last few hours just drift away as if by magic, something that it usually took days of hard training to do. She slept like the dead, that's one of the things I noticed in my midnight vigil that and the fact that she made the sexiest fucking noises in her sleep. I didn't look too closely at the sense of peace I felt standing there looking down at her. By the time I crept from her place in the wee hours of the morning after making some changes to her place I was hard as a rock and suddenly full of energy.

Cierra

I could smell Hank when I woke up in the morning, stupidly I felt around in my bed expecting to find him there until I came fully awake. "Shit now he's following me into my dreams."

I still had the weirdest sense that he'd been here which was a bit unnerving because there's no way that he could've been without me knowing. I found myself checking the house looking for any sign of an intrusion and finding none, yet still I couldn't shake the feeling of his presence. I shrugged it off and tried to throw myself into the rest of my day, tonight was my big date with the man himself there wasn't much for me to do in the way of preparation since I'd already studied him inside and out. I refuse to cart myself off to a spa to get all glamorized for him no matter how much my girlish heart wanted to so I spent my morning and afternoon working on my own little secret investigation.

The question of the murderer's true intent had been raised time and again back then because nothing had been taken from the house that night we hadn't had much to begin with. The original investigators had found it hard to believe that he had just simply chosen a house at random and just gone in and slaughtered the occupants. They'd always suspected that there was something else involved, both my parents' backgrounds had been dug into excessively and even my little brother's but nothing had sent up a red flag.

There were no business deals gone wrong, my parents didn't do dugs and had no known affiliation with anything to do with the criminal element or anything else that would bring something like that to their door and so the case had gone cold. Over the years others had taken a stab at it

232 | CATCH ME IF YOU CAN

but always they'd run into that brick wall. When I was old enough to ask questions and be shown what they had so far I'd combed the files repeatedly looking for clues but with no results either.

In the past few years I'd taken to looking for like crimes in the area with no luck, it's as if someone really had just randomly chosen my family but something inside of me wouldn't let me accept that. I went over once again what the investigators had found that night. The way he'd gained entrance, who he'd killed first, the way he'd killed them. All three had had their throats cut, clean cuts by a steady hand apparently.

I still had my dad's old hard drive, every once in a while I'd gone through it looking for clues but there was nothing there but work related stuff from his job as a computer technician. He'd been one of those people who went around to businesses fixing their systems, at the time he'd been killed I remember him saying that we were finally going to be able to move out of the shitty neighborhood we lived in, things were just looking up. That more than anything stayed with me always, that hope he'd had as he'd swung me around spinning dreams of ponies and dollhouses.

I put it away after hours of collecting notes for my already overflowing pile collected from years of doing this, the case might be catching dust on a shelf in a police evidence room in Baltimore but for me it was always in the forefront of my mind and always will be until I could put it to rest.

A call came in hours before our meet and two of the men on him dropped in on me, apparently there were quite a few unaccounted for hours in Mr. Mancini's night. The Intel was sketchy at best but it was considered of great interest when such a thing occurred because it was usually followed by the disappearance of someone. Where and how the bureau had first came up with this analogy was anyone's guess but like I said before someone high up has a hard on for this guy.

Yet with all the speculation and suspicion surrounding him we were sorely lacking in any concrete evidence to substantiate these claims. Now I'm being told to try to find out where and what he'd been up to for those missing hours. I'm beginning to think that my colleagues really have no idea who they were dealing with, the fact that they're asking me to do these things shows that they didn't understand how he operated at all.

My one night with him had further opened my eyes to what we were dealing with; Hank Mancini was not a man to be easily led, he wasn't going to be swayed by my beauty and charm and though I got the feeling that he was definitely interested I didn't think for a minute that it would change that fact, that just made my job that

much more difficult. The guy was
going to be a hard nut to crack.

Durant called ten minutes before I was headed out the door.

"Stone you ready for tonight?"

"Yes sir I've got everything in place. I made sure to pick a place that our guys could have access to. Our table will have eyes and ears on it the whole time and his shadow will be on-site." That was one for the win column, since we weren't allowed to tap any of Hank's places or the man himself the fact that I could get close to him eliminated the legal aspects. In essence it was entrapment yes, but there were loop holes a mile wide that we could skate through, I left such things to the organizers.

If we got burnt once more none of this will fall back on me, I'm just an agent doing the job she was assigned to. It was spectacularly confusing how they'd worked it out in their minds but hey if it worked none of that will matter; I got butterflies in my stomach at the thought, the truth is I was becoming less and less hopeful of it working. I'd accepted sometime in the last day or so that I wanted him to win, that I didn't want him to be the criminal mastermind they suspected him of being.

A very precarious if not dangerous turn of events; I also accepted that my excitement at seeing him again had more to do with my attraction to him as a man and less to do with the job. I was now walking a very tight rope of uncertainty but couldn't seem to control the feelings he'd awakened in me; they just added another layer for me to peel away.

"Good, good, how do you feel, ready to beard the lion in his den?"

I had to roll my eyes at that sce, no clue whatsoever as to the true nature of this guy.

"I'm ready to do the job sir."
Liar.

"Good woman, try to get some more insight into this guy see what makes him tick, so far we're batting a thousand and I can't stress enough how much we need something."

No pressure though.

"Sure sir I'll do my best."

I was surprised at how easily I shed my nervousness in its place was an excitement at seeing him again. I wondered what outlandish things he'd say to me tonight or would he play the smooth operator? I made sure I got there ahead of him I'd already spotted my cover, the fact that I was able to find them that easily only meant that someone as sharp as Hank probably would too; hopefully he'd just think they were there on him and had nothing to do with me.

He had to be accustomed to having a man on him by now, he's been aware of our presence for almost a decade and had in fact fought and won a few cases against us for violation of his privacy which is why the team was even now sitting the required distance away as was ordered by the judge. No doubt that stuck in the craw of the one who was after him.

Chapter 13

Mancini

Did they have to be so fucking obvious? I mean seriously, after all this time you'd think they'd have upped their game. They might as well have been wearing a sign that said G-men. She on the other hand was looking exceptionally pretty in her off the shoulder blouse, which is all I could see of her outfit from my vantage point across the room. Her hair fell in curls to her shoulders and I noticed her little butterfly pin slash camera, was pinned to her blouse again.

I approached with an air of nonchalance even though I had no doubt the place was bugged to pick up even the fall of lint from my cuff if there was any. I flashed my boyish grin to unnerve her as soon she caught sight of me. I've been told that it's very disarming to the opposite sex. Watching that blush spread from her cheeks to her shoulders, I was reminded of what she looked like when I watched her in her bed the night before. Sweetly innocent and yet so fucking alluring, it won't be long now, I could feel the burn in my gut the need that wouldn't be assuaged until I'd taken her. I had the feeling that when I did finally have her beneath me it was going to take a very long time to slate my lust.

"Good evening Cierra."

"Hank."

She seems a little more nervous than the other night and I wondered if it was because of our audience or her natural reaction to me the man?

"So how are you finding our fair city? Visited the shops as yet?" I took my seat across from her.

"I've done some shopping yes."

No you haven't you spent the first part of the day with your colleagues trying to figure out where and what I did last night. My easy smile gave nothing of my inner thoughts away, picking up my menu I scanned our surroundings from beneath my lashes they might be more than one variable here after all and it always paid to be careful.

Cierra

After a pretty awkward start the evening progressed rather smoothly, he'd pretty much demolished my feeling of calm with his first smile and it had taken me a while to get back on even footing and I was finally able to put on my professional cap and remember why I was here. Maybe having ears and eyes on me helped keep me focused whatever it was I was grateful, I had a hard enough time keeping things light. There were times when it seemed Mancini was playing games, he kept making a point of being suggestive, not that he was overly lewd or anything like that no he's too much the gentleman for that, but it seemed he was trying to get under my skin with every word.

"So what is it that you do again Sierra?"

"I'm in acquisitions." I took a sip of my wine to take my eyes off of his, he was looking right into me as if he knew my every secret it was to say the least very unnerving.

"Really what is it that you acquire?" There he goes again with that knowing look and my traitorous feelings were no help either, each time he looked at me like that as if he would like nothing better than to take me right there at the table my heart tripped and my blood heated. I was beginning to realize that he would always have this effect on me, that no matter how much I steeled myself against it, against him he will always make me melt.

I have no real experience with this need I had for him, the feelings he seemed to call forth so effortlessly; he made me question myself. I'd come here with my own doubts as to his guilt to begin with and so far I'd seen nothing to suggest that he was indeed the man they'd painted him to be all these years, instead he was just guilty of knocking my carefully structured world off its axis.

"Things; how about you Mr. Mancini I mean Hank apart from the nightclub business what else if anything do you do? Or is it true what they say about you?"

"And what's that Cierra what is it that they say?"

"Well word around town is that you're a playboy heavy on the play." I finally looked back at him because suddenly I needed to know the answer to this more than anything.

"One shouldn't believe everything they hear it could prove to be a danger."

"Why so ominous?"

"Am I? I thought it was adhering to a known school of thought, it's a very dangerous thing to believe everything you hear without first getting the facts for oneself."

"And what are the facts?"

"A bit personal don't you think especially after you made a point of telling me how intrusive I was the other night?"

Mancini

I watched her as she fiddled with her glass, she was even more beautiful tonight than the last time she'd sat across from me like this and it was difficult keeping the memory of her asleep in her bed at bay. I wondered as I sat there if I would be spending yet another night keeping watch over her as she slept.

"Okay Hank since that's too personal why don't we stick to the mundane? So how was your day Hank, did anything particularly interesting or are you over your hometown already?"

Very slick agent Stone very slick indeed; this line of questioning could only mean that her agency had gotten a whiff of something in the air, too bad they were too lax to pick up the scent.

"Not especially no, you?"

She smiled at me as she prepared to lie, out of the side of my eye I saw one of the dicks in a suit shift in his chair; what didn't they trust their brightest and shiniest new star to handle even a simple sit down? Or was this a case of boys not wanting the girls to play on their team? Under the guise of studying my surroundings I took in their locations, I was pretty sure that I'd found them all when I first entered but you never know.

I had no fear of them doing anything here and now, they had nothing on me after all and the business of the night before could in no way come back to me. The young girls that had been rescued were even now being looked after in a secure location and for some stupid fuck reason I'd asked Wilson for a much-needed vacation. The older man had been stumped to say the least, after all he's been asking me for years to take it

248 | CATCH ME IF YOU CAN

easy but I never accepted the invitation to take some time off not until now.

There was always something that needed doing somewhere, always a fire to put out. This time I decided to be selfish, I wanted to focus all my time on the woman who had drawn me out of my bed in the middle of the night. The one who refused to leave my thoughts for longer than a moment, or two.

I would be no use to anyone anyway if this kept up so it was best to get it out of the way; not that I planned to spend my days mooning over the beauty no, I still had my businesses to oversee, at least they weren't a matter of life or death for some innocent soul. Besides I needed to shake up some things in a few of my places anyway. At least that's the excuse I was giving myself.

"By the way I have some free time coming up and I would love to take you out on my boat."

I could see that threw her a little she wasn't expecting that but I was sure the Fed in her would grab at the opportunity to get that much closer to me. Another coup for her I'm sure they'd see it as that, nothing wrong with making her look good in front of her peers, how she handled failure at the end of the day was an entirely different matter.

I was caught in a very precarious position here, I wanted her, if that want went beyond a nice hard fuck remained to be seen, if it was just an itch that I needed to scratch, no problem, but if it was more than that then we had a problem. There was no doubt that she would be disappointed in her failure to catch me in her web, but how would she deal with that failure? Would it stand in the way of a future for us granted that's what I decided I wanted after all?

"That sounds lovely, thanks for the invite." She took a sip of her wine as she watched me over the rim and just for a second I saw the woman behind the badge, the real woman and what I saw in that split second was enough to make me want to reach over the table and take her lips. Not yet Hank, she's skittish yet; suddenly my spur of the moment decision to take her out on the water seemed like the best idea in the world, a whole day spent out on the water just her and I, her peers wouldn't be able to follow us there it would be too obvious if they followed us out to sea too close, of course there was all types of technology that would allow them to spy from afar but I had ways around that.

"Then its settled I'll pick you up around nine in the morning."

"Wait what, that soon? I thought you meant in a couple of days I might not..."

Yeah and give your people time to come up with something, some way to keep tabs on our day? Fuck no, this day wasn't about our business this was totally personal.

"I'm sorry but it has to be tomorrow I have things lined up all week so, unless you want to cancel...?"

"No, no, tomorrow's fine, I just… I guess I can find something suitable to wear out on the water."

"What's so hard? All that's needed is a swimsuit and maybe a wrap if we stay out late and it gets chilly."

"You're probably right."

Wait did she have a suit? I hadn't even thought of that, I'm sure she hadn't planned for a day on my yacht then again maybe they were so sure of her progress that they'd planned for even that.

We enjoyed a poignant silence while the server brought our meals over; I took the time to study her more fully under the watchful eyes of the men that were scattered around the room. I wondered what they would do if anything if I reached over and kissed her? Were they here to protect her or to keep an eye on me? It pissed me off to think that if I truly was what they suspected me of that they'd send her into danger, I had no doubt they would let her get on that boat with me tomorrow because for them it was all about the end result, it didn't matter that they could be putting her life in danger after all they saw me as a predator, yet they'd sent an innocent little lamb my way.

We exchanged bullshit small talk or more accurately we lied to each other over scampi and later tiramisu and coffee, well I had coffee the agent had tea. I was in turns fascinated and pissed at her, she had an amazing mind and when I wasn't baiting her and she relaxed her guard just a little she was sweet and funny. I was heading into dangerous territory when her tinkling laugh touched off something inside me. I wanted to… no- planned to taste those lips of hers before the night was over.

My smile at one of her references to something in the news was genuine. I too was learning to relax in her presence. As soon as I'd made up my mind where I wanted us to go it had all become so simple. I wanted her under me, the sooner the better and I was about to pull out all the stops to achieve my goal. Was it fair of me to plot her seduction, knowing what she was here for and what that would do to her rep as an Agent? Maybe not, but neither was it fair of her to come into my life to deceive, and entrap me with her beauty. Hopefully once the dust had settled we'd both have licked our wounds and were able to move on.

Tonight I was allowed to walk her to her car, which turned out to be a town car service.

"It doesn't make sense to drive in the city when everything is right there." That was her explanation, which I let slide as it made sense though I was well aware she had a rental in the parking garage not far from the brownstone.

I kissed her lips softly just a peck and felt the halting of her breath before pulling away slightly to look into her eyes. I couldn't resist running a finger gently down her soft cheek.

"So soft." I hadn't meant to say the words out loud and I for sure hadn't meant for her to hear the need in my voice.

'I'll pick you up in the morning, sleep tight beauty."

"Good night Hank." Was that a hint of sadness I heard in her voice, maybe just a little remorse for her deception of me? Or sadness at the evening coming to an end.

I walked away with the sure knowledge that I was going to once again be standing over her bed in the dead of night.

"Fucking sap." I hadn't even kissed her yet and already she had her hooks into me.

Chapter 14

Cierra

I woke up with that same feeling
again, the feeling that Hank had been
here in my room. I couldn't explain it
to myself but it was an overpowering
feeling I relived that moment from the
night before when he'd ran his finger
down my cheek, the look in his eyes as
he did it. If I didn't know better I
would swear he actually felt something
there for that space in time, what that
something was I don't know.

I had to get up and get moving,
nine o'clock will be here any minute
and I still had yet to give Durant my
report, I'm sure the others had
probably given him their surveillance
tapes and our recorded conversations
and he was probably even now
chomping at the bit to give me
instructions on how to use my new in
to draw Hank even farther into the web
I was setting for him.

The more time I spent in his presence though the more convinced I became that we were barking up the wrong tree. He just didn't fit the type and since I was now considered the brightest new star in the profiling stakes I would think they would take my word for it but somehow I didn't think so, someone high up in the agency had made it their mission in life to destroy this man and they were willing to use the agency to do it, did I want to piss this person off so early in the game with just a hunch going with just my gut, or do I play the game and see where it takes me?

My conversation with Durant was short and straight to the point. He didn't quite come right out and tell me to crawl into Hank's bed if that's what it took but the implications were there. I didn't have time to dwell on that though as Hank would be here soon so I got up and got myself ready with butterflies in my stomach.

"It's not a date Cierra, this is your job, this guy could be one of the biggest criminals in the world why do you have to get all moony eyed and girl stupid over him?" Of all the men over the years that had come into my line of vision why did my libido have to choose him? And since I have no real experience with this nonsense how the hell was I supposed to deal with it?

I couldn't call up Gracie who was the only real female friend I had which was sad considering I'd only met her in the last year. I'd gone twenty three years of life pretty much alone, I hadn't accumulated a lot of friends and acquaintances as I'd been too driven, too focused on one thing for much of anything else.

My foster family was about the closest thing to that and we weren't that close, not because the Taylors were horrible to me or anything like that, it's just that by the time I'd been placed with them after two years in the system I'd already built up my shell. I'd started from the day I watched my family being buried and hadn't stopped ever since. They'd been kind enough, an older couple Michele and Don who couldn't have children of their own, they'd seen that I was fed and had clean clothes and a roof over my head but I'd rebuffed every attempt of theirs to get close. I'd already had a family and lost them I didn't need another one; besides I had a job to do and no one else played a part in that.

I chose a white one piece French cut bikini with a light blue silk wrap for later and covered it with capris and a light cotton button down, I slipped my feet into a pair of flats and hoped like hell they were good enough since I hadn't come prepared with boat shoes.

By the time my doorbell rang I was a nervous wreck.

"Hel..." I didn't get the word out because the man standing at the door looked me up and down and then forced me back inside.

Before I could ask him just what he thought he was doing, I found myself pushed against the wall and his mouth was covering mine. I think my mind left my body. Clichéd, I know, but true all the same. He consumed me, there was no other word for it, his tongue was in my mouth and then it wasn't and he was drawing mine out, his hands, merciful heavens his big strong hands, one was in my back pulling me closer while the other held my cheek in place while he plundered.

I think I remembered how to breathe but vaguely, there was a storm brewing inside my body one that I had no control over. He didn't kiss me, I don't think this is what I remember a kiss to be, no, this was more like a devouring. When he was through making me long for more he took soft little nibbles of my lips that were just as potent as the heated kiss had been.

"Fuck."

"I'm sorry?" His harsh expletive brought me back from the dream world, he didn't answer just studied me curiously as if trying to find the answer to something. His hand came up again and he rubbed my cheek with his thumb.

'You're proving to be very dangerous little beauty."

"What, what does that mean?" My heart was beating out of time, had he somehow figured out what was going on was he onto me?

"Leave it for now baby, you ready?"

I nodded my head stupefied a man had just called me baby and he was still upright, what the hell had happened to me since coming to this city? No not the city, since sitting across the table from this enigmatic man.

All the way to the pier where his boat was docked I was on pins and needles but who could blame me? That kiss was… something, I could still feel the sensation of his lips on mine, his tongue, oh boy. Maybe I should've paid more attention in the past because I had no idea how to swim in these waters. As if I wasn't confused enough as it was that kiss just threw me into even more dangerous territory and what did he mean by that crack anyway how was I a danger to him?

"Why so quiet beauty?"

I turned to look at him from my seat in his high powered sports car, some European number that it would take me two lifetimes to be able to afford no doubt, the man did like his toys.

"Just trying to figure out what you meant earlier when you said I was a danger."

"I told you to leave it alone yeah? It's noting for you to worry about."

"That's easier said than done, now I'll be worried about it all day so why not just tell me?"

"Soon, I promise for now let's just enjoy the day ahead, I hope you like seafood I packed us a lunch." He smoothly changed the subject.

"I love it thanks."

"So did you find another venue for your party as yet? I can ask around for you if you'd like."

Was it my imagination or did he say that kind of tongue in cheek?

"I'm still looking thanks but not to worry I'm sure I'll find something soon."

"Let me know if I can help you out if things don't work out the way you want."

"Thanks." Why did I feel so crummy for deceiving him all of a sudden? He's the one into nefarious dealings after all, and it was my job to get to the bottom of those dealings and bring him to justice if need be but suddenly it didn't feel so right. I felt like a snake which made no sense whatsoever, I've never had a problem before so why should I feel this way with this particular man? I was afraid I knew the answer to that one all too well.

Mancini

She's sweating in her seat, it's probably not very well done of me to bait her like this but the perverse side of me could do no less. I wanted her to regret every moment she spent deceiving me, by the time I had her under me I wanted her willing to put aside everything but the need for me. I will settle for no less, because in the early hours of the morning while I'd stood watch over her bed I'd made a very lasting decision, hard or soft, the woman sitting next to me was mine, I planned to possess her completely and nothing or no one was going to stand in my way.

I didn't question why I felt so strongly about it, didn't have to; the instinct that had been leading me my whole adult life was screaming at me that this was it, she was my one. Why that should be I don't know, after all

I'd met less dangerous women in my time, women who weren't out to put me in a cell and throw away the key. At least it would be something to tell the grandkids somewhere down the line.

Standing over her, wanting to touch her and feeling that pull that was ever present where she was concerned was all the answer I needed to my question of why. Why this woman? It was a cluster fuck for sure, she being who she is, but I'd be damned if I'd let the FBI take anything from me, especially her. No fucking way I haven't fought them this hard for this long to let them rob me of what might be the most important thing to happen in my life.

"So tell me Cierra how is it that someone as gorgeous and smart as you are is still single?"

"I could say the same of you."

"Yeah but it's different for me, we tend to get hitched later in life whereas the female of the species start seeking hearth and home much sooner; so what's your story?"

"Nothing to tell really I've just always been more focused on other things, I guess it's just not that important to me right now."

'I guess that's understandable, what're you twenty two twenty three?"

"Almost twenty four."

Quite young for her current position in the bureau, usually only seasoned veterans held those kind of posts it's my understanding it took years on the job to even reach Special Agent status and even longer to be termed a 'profiler' though the bureau didn't necessarily use that term. My research so far has shown a higher than usual IQ as well as an aptitude for studying and understanding the human psyche.

She was also lauded for her ability to see through the person she was studying; apparently while everyone else saw one thing she saw another. Or at least that had been the fanciful report from one of her old professors. People she'd worked with in the past with the organization she was still a part of that worked to overturn wrongful convictions had nothing but praise and admiration for her.

"So you do see marriage and a family in your future." Not that it mattered one way or the other, I'm sorry to say but when I decided I wanted something there wasn't much that would stand in my way of getting it. The fact that we'd just met meant very little to me, I'd made life-threatening decisions in less time. I wasn't too worried about her thoughts on the matter, again not the most politically correct stand to take but she'd brought herself into my orbit, she shouldn't be too surprised to find herself scorched by the fire.

Chapter 15

The water was calm and serene as we headed out. I think she was still in awe of the beauty of the vessel, and it was a thing of beauty if I do say so myself, my pride and joy or one of many.

"Let me show you around shall I?"

"Sounds good, this is amazing, do you usually just take a yacht out on the water for a day out? I would think these were for longer voyages or something."

"That's the beauty of ownership, you can do as you please with what's yours."

She tilted her head at me, those eyes of hers burning into me, did she have any idea how much I wanted to fuck her right his minute? The only thing keeping me human is the fact that I had not yet ascertained how I was going to handle her deception; do I let her know that I knew who she was, or do I let the farce play out until they realized they couldn't catch me? Whatever decision I came to will have to be soon because it wasn't going to be long before the need to have her under me, to be buried deep inside her overruled everything else.

I showed her around the five hundred and sixty foot vessel with its library, water jets a private cinema and garden among other things. She was quiet the whole time as she followed me from room to room until we reached the six thousand square feet master suite on the topmost deck. Everything had been glossed to a high shine and I enjoyed her reactions as if seeing the place for the first time through her eyes.

"It's truly amazing, really." She ran her hand along the polished teak of the rail as we made our way back below. I'd been on the lookout for her colleagues and hadn't been able to find their location as yet. My yacht was highly secured, bullet and bombproof and according to where we were on the vessel, there were security shields in place to keep us hidden if need be.

"Would you like some breakfast beauty? I know I got you up rather early and it's going to be a long time 'til lunch so if you'd like I can wrestle you up an omelet in the galley."

"You cook?"

"Of course, I'm an excellent cook."

"Fine I'll take you up on that offer since you did get me up so early."

She seemed relaxed as she followed me down I sat her at the island before kissing the crown of her head which seemed almost natural. I meant to use today as part of my campaign to break down her defenses, first I planned on getting her use to my touch, soft touches throughout the day and more stolen kisses.

That kiss had blown me away, it had ben sweet and hot and everything I'd been imagining all morning; I hadn't known I was going to do it though, had anticipated waiting until I'd had her cornered on the yacht before making that first move but she had looked so good standing there, her hair pulled back with a scarf that matched the top she wore, her lips glossed, no makeup that I could see except maybe for a dusting of powder or whatever the hell it was that women wore these days. She had an air of innocence about her that I only noticed when I wasn't thinking of the special agent. When she'd opened the door my mind had still been on what she'd looked like when I slipped out of her bedroom this morning so she'd caught me completely off guard.

I chopped some vegetables for her omelet as I boiled the water to make her some tea, I'd noted the brand

JORDAN SILVER | 273

she favored the night before and was lucky enough to find some in one of those high end overly expensive all night markets in the city. When I placed the cup in front of her I saw her face light up in surprise.

"How did you know?"

"You ordered it last night."

I went back to chopping as she sipped my mind wandering for the time being to her job, I knew from the eyes and ears I'd placed in her place that they suspected me of doing something on the night of the rescue but once again they had no clue where to turn. The inquiry into the car explosion had come up empty and it was ruled an accident; the arrests of the other players were already under way and I'm sure they might eventually be able to put the pieces together but by then it would be too late, besides what were they going to say?

We were still working on the girls' families doing last minute checks to make doubly sure that they weren't going back into danger, I still had one more thing left to do there and it was proving difficult. So far none of the girls were able to give an accurate description of the ones who'd taken them, which was of great concern to us. Before we could send them back we had to eliminate the danger and we couldn't if we didn't know what we were looking for.

I'd tried to ascertain who it could be by using my contacts in that part of the world without much luck, believe it or not trafficking of young girls was not as rare as some might think. Families have been known to sell their children for a profit so it was for me the most delicate part of the operation. Rescuing them had been the easy part, keeping them safe was a whole other story and I knew that when the few days that I'd begged off was at an end I will have to leave her and head to the orient whether we found something or not, sometimes it was better to have your ear to the ground you learned more that way.

"Are you angry at the onion?"

Her question brought me back to the present and I smiled at her teasing tone.

"No why do you ask that?"

"You were scowling at it that's all."

'Nope, had something on my mind."

"Oh, am I keeping you from something?"

'No beauty, I invited you remember?"

"I know but something might've come up I'd totally understand."

Was she fishing or did she genuinely think something had come up? I was more inclined to believe the former, as my beauty seemed to be very efficient at keeping her mind on her job. Yet another thing to punish her for later, my cock twitched at the thought.

I poured the egg mix over the simmering vegetables in the pan and adjusted the heat.

"Nothing's come up, and besides if something had I still wouldn't have cancelled I'm looking forward to spending the day with you doing one of the things I love most."

I turned back to the stove and flipped her omelet over before putting a couple slices of bread in the toaster.

When it was all ready I placed everything neatly on a plate and took it over to her.

"Wow this looks and smells amazing." She smiled up at me and I couldn't help it, I lowered my head and once again kissed her beautiful lips. This kiss was even more heated than the first, my mouth knew the treat it was in for this tine and went in search of her tongue, I played with it running mine over it drawing it into my mouth and sucking on her gently. I had her almost all the way off the stool and in my arms her body held tight against mine as I fought not to fuck her right there in the galley of my ship.

I pulled away with soft kisses across the bridge of her nose and her eyes.

"Eat before it gets cold."

She sat quietly for a moment before picking up her fork and digging in.

Her eyes closed in pleasure after the first bite and she made appreciative noises in her throat.

"Thanks Hank this is good."

"You're welcome."

"Aren't you having any?"

"Nope, not really a breakfast person." I waved the cup of coffee I held in my hand towards her.

"This is as much as I have in the mornings."

She wiped her mouth with one corner of the cloth napkin I'd laid next to her plate before looking at me again.

"I can't seem to get a handle on you, Mr. Mancini."

"Oh yeah why is that?"

"I don't know you seem like such an enigma, supposedly you're this hardcore player with not a care in the world, but here you have this fantastic hidden skill, you're rather courteous when you're not trying to be shocking." She shrugged her shoulders.

"I don't know nothing seems to fit."

"I'm sure you'll figure it out beauty."

Up on deck it seemed like the most natural thing to stand behind her with my hands over hers as I taught her how to man the ship. There was shared laughter and lightness almost as if she' forgotten that I was a job, that she was supposed to be gathering information on me and I stopped waiting for her to try catching me out there.

All in all it was a beautiful day spent with an amazing woman that stole herself deeper and deeper into my heart as the time went by. By the time it was time to return I had been convinced that she was the one who would indeed sit next to me at Juliet Mancini's dinner table. My problem now was ending the game, did I come right out and tell her that I knew who she was or do I wait for her to tell me? And would that day ever come?

"I want to see you again soon."

I had her backed up against the same wall as this morning, my hands holding her face up to mine as I kissed her forehead, her cheeks every place I could find, without waiting for an answer I took her mouth with mine pulling her body close letting her feel my need for her. She melted into me her arms coming up and around me as she gave herself over to me.

When I needed air I picked my head up and looked down into her eyes.

"I know you have an issue with my bluntness as you put it, but I think I should warn you, I'm going to take you soon, if you don't want that you should stay away from me and even then I'm not sure I would let you go." I took one of her hands and led it down to my stiff cock, which was beginning to hurt like fuck.

"Feel what you do to me." She looked up at me a little warily, no doubt wondering how she was going to pull this off, she had a job to do and I'd just told her in essence that if she wanted to do that job she'd have to let me fuck her. I wasn't too torn up about it though.

I left her after stealing another kiss. I felt lighter somehow having gotten that off my chest. At least it was out there, now she had to think about it. I was almost certain that she wouldn't fuck me to further her agenda so I felt sure that if or when she came to my bed she would be there because she wanted to be there.

Cierra

I was a ball of confusion after he left, my nerves were shot and I had butterflies in the pit of my stomach; why would he throw me a curve ball like that? And better yet how the hell was I supposed to handle it? I've worked really hard to get where I am, could I risk throwing it all away for what might be nothing more than a fling? I know I didn't believe him guilty of the crimes we suspected so as a woman I had no guilt there but as an agent tasked with a job would it be unethical to go there with him? I wish I knew the answers to my questions.

I paced the apartment for the next hour or so in deep thought; was this something I wanted? Was he even giving me a choice? Was the attraction I felt for him enough to risk what I would most certainly be risking? I'm sure my boss wouldn't mind me sleeping with Hank to garner more info to put him away, but that's where I draw the line.

There's no way I could do that, but there was no way I could walk away from everything I'd built up over the years, could I? But what about the way he made me feel? Would I be throwing away a chance at real happiness? Could I have it all? A man who made my heart flutter, my pulse race and still keep my career? I didn't see how, there was no way it could work. The thought made me sick to my stomach. Why did it have to be him?

There were no easy answers as I walked back and forth my mind in turmoil, how had my life spiraled out of control so quickly? In just a few short days I'd gone from knowing who I was and what I wanted to this. Now everything I'd thought I wanted seemed threatened, each time I thought of the job I saw his face the way it looked after he kissed me, or felt his hardness under my hand. I kept going round and round in circles but still there were no easy answers, either I gave up the chance to find out if there could be anything there with this amazing man, or I risk my job and reputation as a serious agent. It was a no win situation and once again Hank Mancini had struck, they didn't call him the career ender for nothing.

Chapter 16

Mancini

I watched her pacing and knew that it was I who'd done that to her but there was nothing to be done for it. If I'd read her right and I believe I have, then she felt something for me. What that something was is still left to be seen but there was no going back. Once I made up my mind I forged straight ahead there was no point in wasting time now was there? I had a few more days left of down time and then I'll most likely be on a plane to Asia leaving her behind for at least a few days, there was no way I was doing that without taking her first.

I guess my brothers were right after all when the right woman got her hooks into you she could make you fuck stupid, I know I have no right sniffing around her, she was a part of

286 | CATCH ME IF YOU CAN

everything I hated, I had no doubt part of her dilemma right now the biggest part I'm sure was her job, she wouldn't want to risk that not with the reasons she'd fought so hard to get there still unresolved. I can and will help her find her family's murderer when the time comes but for now she had a tough decision to make, one I couldn't make for her. Was it presumptuous of me to think she might even go there on such short acquaintance? No I don't think so, I'd felt her need, I'd seen the wanting in me reflected in her.

I touched the screen where she was now sitting with a cup of her favorite tea while she gazed off into space.

"Go to sleep baby."

She got up from the chair and went into her room where I thought she was actually about to follow my unheard orders but she was soon back with a little metal box that she placed on the table before her. I knew the contents even before she started digging through them and pulling stuff out one by one. I kept my eyes on her as she wept over the pictures of her family; I was halfway out of my chair when the first tear fell and out the door before she'd made the first sound.

I didn't think about what I was going to say to her once I got there, didn't think of an excuse to give her, I just knew the sight of her sitting there so all alone weeping was more than my heart could take. I'd already made up my mind and whether she knew it or not she was mine there was no way I could leave her like that.

I was ringing her doorbell fifteen minutes later, when she answered I could see she'd done a good job of removing any sign of tears from her face but not good enough I could still see the remnants. Without uttering a word I picked her up and walked inside with her held tightly in my arms, if she questioned how I knew where her bedroom was later I'd deal with it but right now I didn't care. I didn't care who she was or what she was doing here, I just needed to be with her, needed to erase the picture of her sitting there alone in a dark apartment looking so lost and alone from my mind. I understood fully the depths of her turmoil when she didn't say a word to stop me, just laid her head against me as if she knew nothing was going to stop me from taking her.

She was quiet while I laid her back across the sheets and started to undress her, quiet when I ran my hands over her partially clothed body, and when my lips met hers she ignited. The kiss was hot and wet and wild, she seemed hungry, in need; I reveled in the heat of her as she rubbed her soft skin against me. Her little hands were shaking as she fought with the zipper of my pants and I helped her release me into her hands. Fuck her hands on me felt amazing. I pulled my shirt off over my head and went back to her crushing her body beneath mine as I took her nipple into my mouth and sucked. I knew this first time was going to be rough and wild, the soft care will have to come after for now nothing mattered more than getting inside her.

"I'll make this up to." I felt her with my fingers, easing them in and out of her until she was moist and open, her cunt tight around my fingers as I pushed them deeper and deeper into her. Her hips rocked up to mine and I added another finger while gritting my teeth the whole time forcing myself to go slow when all I wanted to do was plunge my cock into her. I could feel myself leaking against her leg as I worked my mouth down her body until I reached her core and buried my nose in her heat inhaling her sweet scent. I licked in between the crease of her thighs before opening her up for my tongue.

My first taste of her went through me, nothing had ever tasted this good, she writhed and moaned against my mouth as I ate her sweet pussy like a starving man, I sent my tongue deeper still within her as I lifted her ass bringing her closer to me. Her hands grabbed fistfuls of my hair as she fucked my tongue and her sweet voice pleading for release was almost more than I could bear. Without waiting any longer I reared up and surged into her. Fuck she wasn't supposed to feel this good, nothing ever had before. I stayed buried inside her for a few minutes while getting us both accustomed to my length inside her. Her small pussy fought to accept all of me as she settled around me.

"Look at me Cierra." She opened the eyes she'd closed in pleasure and stared up into mine remnants of her earlier tears made them bright but now there was lust there as well.

"It's going to be okay, everything's going to be fine I promise." She made a small cry as I plunged into her going as deep as I could reach inside her. Amazing, she felt so fucking good wrapped around me finally and everything else just melted away, the sweet rush of heat that coated me when her pussy twitched around me was sweet salve for my soul.

I nuzzled her until she turned her lips up to mine and I ravaged her mouth with my tongue and teeth, nipping her swollen bottom lip as I kept up a steady in and out fucking into her sweet warmth. Fuck who knew she would feel this good? That she would fit under me as if made to be there when no one else ever had. No one else had ever fitted my cock so perfectly, the way she grabbed me and moved around me, the way she dug her nails and heels into me begging me without words to plunder her pussy.

I looked down at her in wonder and thought this was happening, it was really fucking happening as I felt my heart give over to her so easily, so simply. Fuck, what the fuck?

The way she held onto me like a vise grip, the way her pussy walls clenched around me but most of all, the look in her eyes told me that for all her past experience she was new to this. Her body strained up to mine seeking, seeking as she keened and mewled while I fucked her hard and deep.

I felt the need to cum and yet didn't want it to end not yet I wanted to stay inside her forever. I sped up my thrusts as the need to mark to claim overtook me. I had no idea what was happening to me as my heart and mind joined together as one with one accord, I had to make her mine now. I bit into that place where her neck met her shoulder as I fucked her to climax her silken walls dragging me over the edge with her making me cum harder than I ever have before.

"You feel fucking amazing, just like I knew you would." I uttered those words as I rolled to the side bringing her with me.

"I'm staying the night in the morning we'll talk." I pulled her into my arms and held her close until we both slept.

In the morning we didn't get that chance to talk as my phone went off in the wee hours with a message from Wilson, it looks like my job wasn't over after all. The faction in Asia responsible for the kidnappings was now thought to be part of an international child trafficking outfit with cells in Asia and Eastern Europe and as far down as Central America.

It was bigger than we had first thought and my little vacation was going to be cut short. Fuck, this couldn't have happened at a worst time I'd just taken her for the first time and everything in me demanded that I stay and solidify that bond. There hadn't been enough time spent claiming her, marking her making her one hundred percent mine.

Now I was being made to leave her with so much left undone between us. I've not had time to inspect these strange new feelings she brought out in me, not yet explored the newly awakened feelings of having to own completely, oh well, there was nothing for it, was there? I had a job to do, numerous children's wellbeing was at stake here and that wasn't something I could turn my back on so easily. We'll have to settle things once and for all once I got back which hopefully wouldn't be too far in the future.

"I have to leave for a little while something came up." I put my finger across her lips before she could ask any questions, I'd been fully prepared to come clean this morning, to tell her I knew who she was but now I wasn't so sure that that was such a good idea, not when I had to leave her.

"We'll talk when I get back, promise me you'll be here." She looked up at me with just a hint of fear in her eyes whether that fear stemmed from what had happened between us last night and the ramifications to her job or from something else I did not know, I just knew I wanted it gone.

"Promise me Cierra, don't make me have to come looking for you baby." I shook her a little until she gave me her consent.

"I'll be here I promise." She still didn't sound too sure but I let it pass, I had already made up in my mind to have my brothers looking out for her while I was gone anyway so there was no way she could disappear on me.

"I have two brothers both of whom will be coming to see you after I'm gone, sorry I have to do it this way I thought there would be time to introduce you later but it looks like there's no time."

"Why do I need to meet your brothers while you're gone?" She knitted her brow in confusion and maybe just a little consternation after all she had to know that Adrien and Jaxxon were part of her organization though they were years ahead of her and had no reason to know who she was.

"Because I need them to look after you when I'm gone."

"I don't need looking after Hank. That's silly, I'm a big girl, I can take care of myself."

"That may well be but it goes against everything I am to leave my woman unprotected in the city."

"Your...your woman?" I rolled over on top of her and eased into her morning warmth.

"Yes, mine."

THE END

You may contact the author @

Jordansilver144@gmail.com

Jordansilver144.wordpress.com

https://www.facebook.com/MrsJ ordanSilver

amazon.com/author/jordansilver

If you enjoyed this you might also enjoy these works by the author

Taken
http://www.amazon.com/dp/B00FEW
YN7K

The Sweetest Revenge
http://www.amazon.com/dp/B00FAY6
CC6

His One Sweet Thing
http://www.amazon.com/dp/B00F6C5
O0I

And many more, thanks for reading

Made in the USA
Las Vegas, NV
28 January 2025

17116486R00164